It, Watching

Also by Elizabeth Massie:

Sineater

Desper Hollow

Hell Gate

Wire Mesh Mothers

Versailles

The Tudors: King Takes Queen

The Tudors: Thy Will Be Done

Sundown

Afraid

The Fear Report

Homeplace

Naked, On the Edge

Dark Shadows: Dreams of the Dark (co-written with

Stephen Mark Rainey)

Buffy the Vampire Slayer: Power of Persuasion

Twisted Branch (written as Chris Blaine)

DD Murphry, Secret Policeman (co-written with Alan

Clark)

Welcome Back to the Night

The Ameri-Scares series

The Silver Slut adventure series

Homegrown

It, Watching

Elizabeth Massie

Dark House Press
USA

Shadow on your shoulder.

Cold touch of your hair.

Turn, and you see nothing.

But it is surely there.

Watching.

Close behind and watching.

Don't move.

Take care.

Contents

Wet Birds..1

Tintype.. 17

Darla and Gina Try to Keep Out of Debt..........33

Don't Look at Me..49

Sister, Shhh...59

Breathe Me..81

18P37-C, After Andrea Was Arrested.............83

The Darkton Circus Mystery.........................91

The Tree...111

My Treat (poem)..115

Sickle Moon..117

Dust Cover...137

Pisspot Bay..145

Sarah, In the Attic...161

I Have a Little Shadow...................................163

The Well...175

Landfill...179

The Replacement...195

Wet Birds

It hasn't rained for almost six weeks. The grass is brittle as old chicken bones; the air is heavy with dust and the ash stirred up from the bonfire pit when a wind whips past. The sunlight is thick like puss-laced piss; it seems to soak into the earth rather than brighten it. I watch through the tiny window of the backyard shed, observing a feral cat as it sniffs the ground, gobbles up a dried cricket, and then sulks off beneath the old house trailer, its tail down, its whiskers dragging.

I'm lonely. But nobody gives a shit about that but me.

It's early August. There's a birdbath out in the dead grass, and for some reason Julie believes it is important to keep it filled with water from the nearby creek. Chickadees, goldfinches, and sparrows take turns in the water. They wait, watching, clipped around the rim like feathery decorations on a birthday cake, and when one bird flies out another hops in. It's funny, watching them splash. Their wings shudder and flap, they dip their heads in and out. Every once in a while a blue jay comes along and they all scatter. The jay takes his time bathing, like it's a true luxury. Must feel good, to be a wet bird on a day like today.

Everything is so fucking dry. So fucking hot.

There is movement beyond the birdbath, out past the scraggly yard at the edge of the tree line. I glance in that direction, my eyes narrowing. A rustling there among the pines and sycamores, and then a flickering shadow. Could be a fox or rabbit, though we haven't seen a wild animal around for a while now. They've run off up into the mountains because they don't like the smell of death wandering in the woods.

Most likely the movement is one of the living dead sniffing around, sensing live humans nearby. Julie and Martin have a pistol in the trailer with a few bullets left.

They're pretty good at shooting to kill, so if the zombie comes across to the trailer, they'll get him...or her...before the thing can reach the door.

For a while, the living dead didn't show up around here very often. We're really far out in the country. At first, they mainly hung around where bigger pockets of living food were holed up and hiding, like the cities and towns. Like Stanleyville, the town ten miles east of here. But recently, more and more have shown up at the trailer, which is why Sallie, Bucky, and I thought it might be a good idea to head up into the mountains.

Best laid plans, right?

We'd found the abandoned house trailer while driving the unpaved country roads almost a year ago – last September – looking for a new place to smoke our pot and drink our beer. And there it was in all its banged-up glory, sitting on a lumpy plot of land between two thick woods, empty, just waiting for a bunch of teens like us to take it over. No electricity, of course. No running water. The thing is moldy, filled with mice, spiders. There are a couple outbuildings behind the trailer – a toolshed, smokehouse, and a splintery outhouse sitting at a tilt. But in spite of how crappy the place was – is – we thought it would be a damn good party pad. Julie, me, Martin, Bucky, Sallie, and Robin came here every weekend through the fall, winter, and early spring, bringing along our guitars, weed, and whatever beer was cheapest at the Stanleyville Sharp Shopper.

Then on the last weekend in March (it was Martin's birthday that Saturday. "Eighteen?" we chided him. "Getting' old, man! We'll buy you some Viagra and a wheelchair to get you up and get you around!") we drove out here to celebrate with a packed cooler, a baggie of weed and papers, and a box of birthday cupcakes Julie had baked. Sunday morning we were still there but feeling the effects of the party, sitting and lying around on the mouse-chewed sofa and chairs, sucking down the last of the beer, listening to Martin strum a new song he'd written, which pretty was much crap but since it was his birthday and since Martin can teeter a bit on the edge of crazy-mad sometimes, we pretended to like it. After the song, Robin tugged on my elbow and winked. We shuffled to the back bedroom and locked the door.

"I got my black panties on for you, Lyle," she said, snuggling close against my chest. She was warm and smelled a lot better than the trailer did. Like Pabst, pot, and perfume. "Love me?"

I nodded. I did, kind of. As much as any girlfriend I ever had before.

But just as I was sliding my hands up under her sweatshirt, we heard a pounding on the front trailer door. I pulled my hands back and we stared at each other.

The pounding came again. My heart kicked and started to beat faster. Nobody knew we were here. This place was out in bum-fucking-redneck nowhere where even hermits didn't live. Robin and I raced back to the front room to find everybody standing there, bug-eyed, mouths hanging open.

"Who's at the damn door?" I asked.

"Got to be the sheriff," whispered Julie, holding a desperate, trembling finger to her lips. "Somebody told on us, I bet!"

"I didn't hear no car engine," said Bucky.

"I wasn't paying attention," scoffed Martin. "Were you fucking paying attention? Was anybody? Damn it to hell! What's wrong with you all?"

We had our weed and beer and cigarettes – all those things us under-agers aren't supposed to have for some stupid legal reason – spread out on the coffee table and the counter that separated the kitchen from the living room. Bucky scooped up the pot and stuffed it into his shirt but the beer bottles and butts, they were everywhere. And of course, the whole place smelled of what we'd been up to.

The pounding started again, but I noted it wasn't a normal, "hello" or "let me in" pounding but a sloppy, irregular, scratchy-sounding pounding. The trailer rocked with the blows. Then we could hear a muffled, guttural grunting on the other side of the door.

"I bet it's that asshole, Pete," said Martin.

We all hated Pete. He was forty-something and had no friends and always tried to bribe us into letting him come along to our parties. We never let him but he always begged. He had a bad habit of blowing snot rockets and forgetting to zip up his pants after taking a whiz. He was drunk almost all the time and it was a wonder he could find his way from one place to another.

"Hey, Pete?" called Bucky. "That you?"

Another growl, another slam against the door.

"That don't sound like Pete or no sheriff, that's for sure," said Julie. She tiptoed to the window, pulled apart the rusted mini-blinds, and shrieked, "Holy Fuck!" She fell back, tripping over Martin's guitar case on the floor.

Everyone rushed to the window, no one pausing to help Julie up but squeezing against to each other to peek through the blinds. My head was near the bottom of the clump, my chin pressed down on the sill, but I could see who – what – was knocking on our door.

It was some dead guy.

Dead, I was sure, because part of his face was gone and only a single, shattered bone protruded from his shoulder socket. Flies buzzed around his ears, touched the sticky fluids congealed there, then flew away with haste, as if tasting something so disgusting even a fly wouldn't eat it. His skin was tinted a corpse-ish yellow and green, and a few fingers were missing off his right hand. The whites of his eyes were a ghastly, putrid orange.

Bang bang bang bang.

He drove his dead, pulpy fist against the door, as if he sort of remembered how to knock, even though he didn't know why he would. He grunted, growled, slapped his bloated tongue in and out of the slit that was his mouth.

Martin jumped away from the window first. He snatched his rifle from the wall, flipped off the safety. "Get back everybody, this fucking asshole's going down!"

"Martin, don't you dare open that door!" Sallie shrieked.

But Martin, being Martin, did. The dead guy stumbled forward into the trailer and landed on his face. Black, foul-smelling spittle flew. Martin pumped two bullets in the dead guy's back but it didn't do anything but make the dead guy grunt louder. He rolled over awkwardly, his orange eyes blinking, and tried to pull himself up by grabbing the arm of the sofa.

Julie, Bucky, Sallie, and I slammed ourselves against the far wall, sweating, yelling, shaking like drenched dogs as Robin, who couldn't get over to us, hopped up onto the recliner. The chair gave and folded in on her. She crashed to her ass and then bounced out onto the floor. The dead guy, still on his knees, reached out, got hold of her foot and dragged it to his mouth where he took a big bite out of her ankle.

"Lyle!" she screeched, an inhuman sound I'll never forget, but I knew if I went for her, he would get me. Damn! I didn't have a gun, did I? She couldn't blame me, really, could she?

Julie shoved me forward, "Help her, Lyle!"

But I pressed myself back against the wall again, my breath frozen in my lungs, as Martin blew another hole into the guy's back. That didn't faze him; he gulped down Robin's ankle then bit off the rest of her foot. She flopped like a fish, her stub spraying red, then went still. Not dead quite yet. I could see her chest hitching.

Martin yelled and pumped a round into the back of the dead guy's head and that's what did it. That's what killed him. He shuddered, rose up with Robin's toes clamped between his teeth then plopped backward.

None of us moved. We stared at the dead man who was now really dead, then at Robin who was dying. I unlocked then, and dropped down beside her, pulling her up and shaking her to awaken her. Her eyes fluttered, popped open for a moment and closed again. Then she, too, was dead.

"Oh God oh God oh God!" said Sallie.

"What was...what is..." began Bucky, but he couldn't finish, because he'd spun around to throw up on the wall.

We were always into bonfires. There is a lot of room beside the trailer, a grass-bare, shallow pit packed hard with gravel and thick red clay. Bonfires are cool, powerful, fun.

This one wasn't going to be much fun.

Martin and I dragged the doubly-dead guy outside and put a bunch of twigs and old pallets on top of him, doused him with gasoline, and set him on fire. Robin, well, we rolled her up in a blanket and put her in the back of Martin's pickup. We figured we needed to get her back to Stanleyville and her parents' house. Tell them a bear got her or a coyote got her, anything but a dead guy got her. We knew how that would sound. They might think such an insane suggestion would mean *we* had something to do with it.

I didn't cry until I was in the passenger's seat and Martin started the truck engine. I stared out the window so he wouldn't see the tears cutting down my face. He hates shows of weakness. Pisses him off. Through the smudged glass and my blurry eyes I could see Sallie, Bucky, and Julie stirring the flaming chunks of wood and the charred pieces of the dead man around and around, like witches stirring brew.

We weren't quite a quarter-way to town, through the forest, past fallow fields, and over a concrete bridge spanning Widow's Creek, when we saw someone stumbling up the middle of the road ahead of us, coming in our direction, scuffing up gravel.

"Now just who is...?" I began, but Martin cut me off with, "Oh, fuck this shit!" He slammed on the brakes. I flew forward, almost slamming my head into the windshield.

It was another one. Another dead guy, but this dead guy was a girl. She had a hank of red, matted hair on one side of her head; it swung back and forth heavily. There was no hair on the other side, but the scalp was lacerated and glistening with something dark. She limped like her hip was out of joint. She wore only one shoe. Her arms swung like those of an ape. But it was her face, getting closer by the moment, that convinced us she was, indeed, dead. The whites of her eyes were that disgusting, deathly orange. Her jaw snapped open and closed as if on a spring.

"What the fuck is going on?" whispered Martin through his teeth. "What the hell is all this? This is just fucking wrong!"

The woman got closer, zoned in on the truck now, or on us. Her mouth began to open and close all the faster and her arms raised up, fingers clutching.

"It's like she wants to tell us something," I said. "Or she wants to eat us."

Martin jerked the steering wheel, slamming the truck around, knocking into the dead woman with the rear left end, throwing her out of her shoe and down onto the gravel. As I watched in the rearview, the woman got up and started shambling again.

When we got back to the trailer, the bonfire was leveling out. Julie had a shovel in her hands, ready to toss dirt on it when it was all done. Bucky and Sallie had their arms crossed against a cold March breeze. They glanced up at our return, their brows drawn and mouths down in tight frowns.

Martin pulled the truck up to the fire and fell out.

"There's more of 'em!" he yelled, taking Bucky by the arm and shaking it, hard. "We saw another one, another thing like that guy there!" He hitched his thumb in the direction of the fire. "It was a woman this time."

"Can't be," Bucky said. "This guy here, he was just some really sick dude, some insane sick dude who…"

"No!" I said. "He was a dead guy, and –"

"He wasn't!" shouted Bucky. "Dead guys don't just walk around!"

"Zombies do!" said Martin.

"You've watched *Walking Dead* too much," said Bucky.

Martin's let go of Bucky's arm and his fists drew up. "That's right, freak! And it means I know what I'm talking about! It's fucking zombies! That's what that guy was. And that woman we saw on the road, too. While we been out here at the trailer, away from everybody and everything, something happened, dead people started turning into zombies and..."

"There's no such thing as zombies! That's fucking horror movie crap! That's crazy talk!" said Bucky. He shoved Martin hard. Martin punched him in return, a solid crack against Bucky's jaw. Bucky wailed and bowed over into the pain.

But Bucky and the rest of us were convinced Martin was right only a moment later, when we heard noises coming from the back of the pickup. We spun about to see the rolled blanket undulating, twisting around, and then Robin's hand came out, clutching, scrabbling.

We all screamed at the same time.

Robin was buried with one of Julie's bullets in her brain. We didn't burn her like Sallie wanted, because the rest of us felt hinky about burning a friend. Even though we didn't feel too hinky about the shot to her head, being as she was trying to lunge out of the truck bed, growling and grunting, her lips curled back, her jaws open wide, her eyes glowing orange.

So we sat there in the trailer, drinking beer but not tasting it, picking at our knuckles, staring out the window – the blinds were now pulled all the way up so we could see – as the sun began to set over the wilderness. Then Martin said, "I think we should check out how bad it is."

We knew what he meant. He wanted someone to go on reconnaissance to learn how widespread this zombie mess was. Maybe there was only the two of them, only two zombies...the burned up guy and the gray hair woman on the road. Oh, and Robin. Okay, three. Only three.

But maybe there were lots others, all over the place.

Maybe we were stuck in deep shit. Maybe the whole county was. Maybe the whole country.

And we had to know.

Sallie and Bucky reluctantly volunteered. They took Sallie's car, a beat-up blue Civic, arming themselves with Martin's reloaded rifle. That left us with Julie's pistol, but took a bit of comfort in that because she was a great shot. We double-checked to make sure the door was locked. Then we triple checked it. I drank another beer but couldn't taste it. I wasn't in the mood for a joint. I had a feeling being alert would be better than not.

They came back after midnight. The sound of the car and then the loud, crunching sound of the car striking something solid drove us to our feet and to the window, to make sure it wasn't zombies driving a car.

They shouted for us and we let them in then watched as they sat silently on the sofa for a very long minute. At last Bucky said, "We wrecked Sallie's car. Hit that maple down by the road. Car's pretty much a gonner."

Sallie nodded.

"But no matter," said Bucky, "We ain't never going back to Stanleyville."

"They're everywhere in and around town, swarmin' like bees," said Sallie. "All this, in what, two days? How insane is that?"

"How'd it happen?" asked Julie. "How the hell did this happen?"

Martin glared at Julie. His eyes were small and scary. "Who ever knows? Virus? Bacteria? Space pollution? Chemicals? Radiation? Could be any of that."

Julie linked her arm through Martin's but he stalked away, moving to the counter where he stared at the floor and muttered to himself.

"There's still living people in Stanleyville," said Bucky. "We could see 'em in their upstairs windows. Went by your house, Julie, and seen your Mom peeking out her living room window. We drove by Lyle's house and Sallie's house, and lights were on so we're guessing they're okay. But we just kept driving through and out. The...zombies..." (I could tell he had a hard time saying the word after the grief he'd given Martin) "...threw themselves at the car but we floored it. Most of the stores had broken-out windows, schools, too, and churches. Sallie was damn brave. We pulled up to the Sharp Shopper just outside town and she ran in and grabbed up a big bag's worth of canned stuff. But we ain't going back there again. Too dangerous. We have to stay here."

"How the hell long are we supposed to stay here at this trailer?" I demanded. "Are we just supposed to hope our families are okay?"

"Yeah, that's exactly what we're supposed to do," said Martin, still staring at the floor. "'Cause if they aren't dead now, they'll be dead real soon, count on it."

And as much as I hated it, I knew he was right.

I felt like such a fucking coward.

Days passed. Then weeks. Sallie's stash of canned peaches, green beans, and Spam thinned out so we – well, Julie, actually – hunted critters in the woods. They were a lot faster than dead people but she was able to snare some. We used up the rest of the gasoline from Martin's truck and Sallie's smashed Civic, siphoning it into a bucket to use to start fires to cook. The matches didn't last, either. Martin learned how to start fires with the battery from the Civic, and we all learned how to keep fires going, like people in the old days, assigning someone to always be awake to add more bark or sticks. When it rained, we tended the coals inside the old oven. We also kept a fire going in the smokehouse, where we gutted, skinned then smoked the groundhogs and squirrels we managed to kill, using the old, crusted bags of salt that had been left there by the previous owner (thank goodness Julie had a wacky country grandma who not only taught her how to use a pistol but had also taught her how to cure meats). The meats were tough but at least they didn't spoil. Julie wouldn't let us kill birds, though. She said they were heavenly spirits and we best leave them alone.

At first we saw one zombie a week, thereabouts. Then, by early May we saw two or three a week, wandering up the road, veering off toward the trailer. Still a trickle, but clearly the live humans in and around Stanleyville were running out. Julie and Martin shot them cleanly, and we burned them. But our ammunition was dwindling, so Martin decided to hike to the nearest house – a cabin four miles up the road to Stanleyville – and see what he could find.

There was no one there, and the cabin door was bashed open. Dried blood was splattered all over the floor, furniture. He found a broken shotgun in the bedroom. He also found a few hanks of human hair and bits of bone on the bed. There was a box of bullets in a kitchen drawer, which he pocketed for his pistol. He also pocketed the only good food he found – three cans of beets and a jar of olives; the stuff in the refrigerator was beyond spoiled.

On his way home, as it got dark, he spied a zombie out in a field, chewing on an arm. Then he saw another near the first, gnawing flesh from a head. Martin ran most of the way back to the trailer, stumbling several times in his terror, breaking his wrist in the process, and then was sick three days from all the running, his wrist splinted and making him moan even in his sleep.

There were no more animals to hunt by late May, and all the smoked meats were eaten. Now we were collecting dandelion greens, dry land cress, wild asparagus, and berries from the edge of the forest, and trying to trap mice but they were sneaky and knew what we were up to, so rarely got caught. We were weakening from lack of food and a fear of leaving the trailer. Zombies came, were shot and sometimes staked in the head, burned. The stench was dreadful. Not just the zombies, but us.

The first Friday in June, Bucky, Sallie, and I had a talk. We had to get out of there. We would go into the mountains where the wild animals had gone, gather our wits and search for other foods, then move on. Zombies probably stayed away from steeper slopes, as uncoordinated as they seemed to be. We might be okay.

Martin was furious. He got up in my face, grabbed my shirt with his good hand, and swore we better stay put.

"What, and starve to death?" I asked. "Have you seen yourself in the mirror lately? Have you really looked at any of us?"

"Sure, we're starving here." Damn, but Martin's breath was sour. I tried not to make a face or turn away. Didn't want to piss him off anymore than he already was.

"But here you got walls, Lyle. Look around! Walls to protect your sorry ass!"

"We got to do something…"

"And if Julie and I don't go with you, you won't have guns to hunt food, neither."

"We can make snares, traps, maybe."

"Maybe? How many mice you catch with your idiot traps here in the trailer, huh?"

"We can try harder. And we'll cross over the mountains, maybe find some other people…"

Martin's face was red, his eyes dark-rimmed, crazy, and wide. "Zombies'll get you, Lyle. You can bet your fucking ass on that. You'll fall asleep against a tree or a boulder. They'll come up on you before you know it. Bite your heads off, eat the skin like an apple peeling!"

"Martin, listen, if you come with us, you and Julie and the pistol…"

"I could have died out there!" Martin screamed. Julie reached for him but he shoved her away, his splinted arm flailing. "I realized when I was on my way back that one more stumble and I would have been zombie food. Eaten alive! Or eaten partially, and then come back to life like Robin!"

"Okay, okay, we won't go," I said. Sallie and Bucky glared at me and moved to protest, but I waved them to the back bedroom as Julie helped Martin back onto the sofa and wiped his brow.

"We'll leave when he's asleep," I said once were out of Martin's earshot. "He's messed up in the head as it is. No need to make it worse. Julie won't leave him here alone, so we'll go early in the morning, dawn, when we can see but before they're awake."

Sallie was shaking but she nodded. Bucky put his arms around her but the trembling continued. "We'll stay together, no matter what?"

Bucky nodded. "No matter what."

Dawn came after a nightmarishly long night in which I dreamed of dining on raw feet and bloated tongues. Martin was snoring on the sofa; Julie was rolled up in a blanket on the floor beside him. Sallie, Bucky, and I gathered in the hall then moved as stealthily as possible into the living room, holding our breaths, biting our cheeks. The damned front door creaked as we eased it open but neither Julie nor Martin stirred. Out we went then around the side of the trailer where I collected the axe from beside the bonfire pit. Bucky shouldered the shovel and Sallie the rake. We looked like folks going after Frankenstein. Or three of the seven dwarfs, off to work.

Breathing as hard as if we'd run a marathon, we started across the backyard, past Julie's birdbath, sending sparrows in a mad flutter. If nothing else, I told myself, we were trying. If nothing else, we weren't going to die in a trailer, lying on the floor in our own dried-up, mouse-chewed shit.

And then we heard Martin howling, running footsteps, and a loud *pop*! Sallie went down, cold dead, the rake flipping from her hand and red flowering at the back of her head. Bucky and I spun around. Then Bucky was shot in the forehead and crumpled in a lifeless heap.

"Get back here!" Martin yelled. He stood at the corner of the trailer, Julie beside him, her hair caught up in her fingers, unable to make the insanity stop.

I dropped the axe and ran.

A bullet whizzed by my ear but missed. The gun fired again, catching me in the hip, sending red-hot electricity up through my body. My legs buckled out from under me, but I pushed myself upward and kept on running.

Into the woods. Toward the mountain.

I'm not sure how long I was on my feet – seconds? hours? – but my body grew cold and my legs ceased working at some point. I dropped to my knees and then fell flat out in a patch of poison ivy and thorns.

I lay panting, my hip burning, my breath growing shallower with each inhalation. Waiting for death, not caring anymore.

Then I heard a rustling of brush, and a grunt, and my head turned enough to see a zombie struggling through a thicket, his sights trained on me. He was one ugly motherfucker, this dead guy. Ears rotted, ribs showing through a tattered shirt. Ticks in his beard, probably just there for the ride since there was no real blood for them to suck.

I tried to scramble away. I was ready to die but not this way. Becoming zombie food or turning into a zombie myself? *Hell, no!* I tried to cry out but I only squeaked. This seemed to rev up the desperate hunger of the dead guy, who clacked his fuzzy green teeth and shoved himself through the thicket even as hunks of skin were raked from his bare arms.

Oh, shit, oh please no!

He reached down for me, grabbed my hair, hauled me up. His toxic drool splattered on my lips, in my eyes. I blinked and began to sob.

Then a bullet struck his head, splattering bone and fluid, and he let go of me. I heard Martin shout, "Die, bastard!" He could have meant me as much as the zombie. The zombie dropped away, dead for sure now. And Martin was over me, eyes twitching, fingers shoving another bullet into the pistol's chamber.

I opened my mouth to say something, I don't know what, really, and swallowed the zombie's fouled spit as Martin said, "You betrayed me, you shit!" and blew a hole in my chest.

I faded.

I died.

But then I came back. I fucking came back, sort of. Can you believe it? Damn it to hell, I'd rather have been one of the living dead wandering the roads and the forests than what I am now.

After killing me, Martin strung me up in the smokehouse along with Susie and Bucky. He and Julie stripped our bodies, scooped out our insides, stitched our mouths and eyes shut, trussed us, salted us, and then started up the fire in the firebox. Can't waste good meat, not these days.

But I came back. Not mindless like the other zombies, because I am only infected from drool, not from a bite. Funny that these are minor details that really matter. It wasn't that way in *Night of the Living Dead* or *The Walking Dead*, was it? But then again, those are just stories. This is real.

I still have my mind, but it doesn't work like it used to. It won't send signals to my vocal chords or my arms and legs. As much as I want to, I can't make sounds or wriggle. I can only hang here, watching wet birds in the birdbath with the one eye that wasn't sewn tightly enough and popped loose of the threads. I can only feel the heat and the dry and loneliness.

And oh, yes, the hunger. There is that hideous, gnawing agony deep in my bowel-less gut.

I see Julie now. She's in the backyard, standing in the dead grass, one hand in the pocket of her jeans, the other holding a dull knife. She studies the birds on the birdbath from a respectable distance. They make her smile. They are life. Healthy life. Julie, on the other hand, is as far from healthy as you can get without being dead. She and Martin still scavenge dandelions and cress. Asparagus season is long over. I know they've been eating insects, too. I've watched her scoop of spiders and beetles from the ground and pop them into her mouth like Skittles.

Julie leaves the birdbath, unlatches the smokehouse door, squinting against the gray smoke as it billows up around her. She steps inside, pokes at the firebox with a rake, and then adds some chunks of wood and bark. She coughs; it's hot and dry as hell in here. She comes close to me, spins me around on the hook, and frowns. Obviously I'm not ready to consume.

She moves over to Bucky, nods, and slices a long slab from his leathery, well-smoked, meaty thigh, heaves it over her shoulder, and leaves the shed.

When it comes my turn to be consumed, I hope Martin selects my head for a meal. He'll snip away the stitching on my eye and mouth, hold me up to his lips to take a bite.

And I'll bite him first. Oh, you bet. I'll bite the shit out of him. Watch him scream, see the terror in his eyes when he realizes just what lies in store for him.

I watch Julie through the tiny window. Carrying the slab of meat she goes to the birdbath, dips her finger in the water, rubs it on her face, and then disappears around the side of the trailer. Martin will be anxiously waiting for her inside, pacing to all the windows with her pistol, watching for movement on the road, in the trees.

I guess the movement I saw at the edge of the woods was just my imagination. Or perhaps it was the tears blurring my vision. Strange that I still can cry.

I shut my one eye. I feel the wet course down my cheek, and pretend I'm a bird in the birdbath, refreshed and ready to fly away.

Tintype

Oliver O'Donnell sweated heavily at night, even in the colder months, because evening was too silent, too dark, and that was the time that memories – the worst of them all, the most foul and intimate and dreadful – jeered and paraded over the bare walls of his tiny room or across the backs of his closed eyelids.

War was hell. General Sherman had made that clear. He'd written, "Some of you young men think that war is all glamour and glory but let me tell you boys, it is all hell!"

But for Oliver, still a young man at twenty, it wasn't war that was the greatest of all hells, for war had an end to it. Rather, it was the weeks that followed the war. The months after last cannon was fired, the last bloodied soldier hit the ground, the last man stumbled free from a prisoner of war camp. Yes, that was hell. The time after. When one could think. Was forced to remember over and over again. To marvel in horror what he had seen, what he had done.

The late November wind was fierce. It howled through the street below like a banshee seeking the next to die. It shook the shutters and window glass of Oliver's grimy fourth floor Philadelphia boarding house room.

Oliver lay on his cot, hands clasped to his chin, breathing hard, staring at the ceiling. There, too, the dreaded memories danced. Danced and taunted, leered with grit-crusted eyes and threatened with skeletal fingers that clicked like bits of tin. Oliver shook his head and dug at his eyes, but the visions remained.

Accusatory grins filled with blood-stained teeth.

Oliver rolled off his cot, kicking the blanket away, and walked to the window. There he leaned, panting, his forehead against the glass. He watched as dead leaves spun about in macabre, air-borne pirouettes and stars winked accusingly in the distant blackness. Two blocks away, beyond the roofs of shorter buildings, he could see the moon's reflection on the Delaware River. Ripping, undulating, damning.

"It will never leave me," he whispered, his breath fogging the pane. "My sins will never be forgiven."

Turning back, Oliver shuffled to the caned chair by the bed. He sat and looked at his shoes, overturned on the floor. They still bore the mud of Georgia. No matter how many times he'd scrubbed them, it remained.

The memories remained.

#

He was captured at the Battle of Mansfield and transported with thirty-seven of his fellows to the Camp Sumter prison in Andersonville in April of 1864. What he saw as he entered the gates of the stockade with his fellow Union soldiers froze the blood in his veins.

The prison was little more than a huge outdoor corral for human beings, surrounded by a tall and solid wooden enclosure. Mud. Flies and mosquitoes as heavy as fog. A central, rancid swamp in which human feces floated and rats swam. Moldy tents, both issued and makeshift. Mounds of debris. And most horrific of any sight possible – men who were no more than skin stretched over bone, men shuffling about with eyes sunken back and away from reality, some nearly naked and others completely so, dotted with welts and sores and streaks of diarrhea down their pitiable legs.

"Heaven have mercy!" said Robert, a freckle-faced redhead from the 48th Ohio regiment, and Oliver's best friend since joining up in January. "We're going to die here. Would that I have been hit by a ball in the forehead and died on the spot!"

"Don't say that," said Oliver, though he was thinking the same. "We'll get out of here soon. We aren't going to end up like…" he cocked his head in the direction of one man, naked, lying in the mud like a corpse dug up from a grave, yet still breathing. "…like him."

"Oh, yes, we will," said Robert. "Ain't nobody gonna get out of here alive!"

"Shut your mouth, Robert. We will. We will."

Robert grabbed Oliver's sleeve. His eyes were wide, terrified. "How, tell me! How, when this is Hell itself?"

Oliver didn't know. His gut was so knotted, his mouth so dry, and his mind so twisted that he could only utter what he wanted to be true but knew could not be true. "We will. We will."

He and his compatriots were given seven tents and a tiny spot of ground near the swamp on which they would live until the war's and. If they lived.

The first days were excruciating, thirty-seven men trying to make a camp for themselves amid the stench and squalor without losing the little they'd been allowed to keep by the guards – canteens, boots, tin cups, belts, caps. One particular hoard of inmate marauders, nicknamed the "Raiders," had survived by perfecting their thieving. Wielding clubs, they attacked anyone who had something they wanted, and either scared it out of them or beat it out of them.

Oliver earned a brutal scar on his left leg when the Raiders attacked their pathetic little campsite by the swamp on the third day. He had given up a small tintype of his mother (why the Raider had wanted it, Oliver couldn't fathom, except perhaps the grizzled man had merely enjoyed the pain he saw in Oliver's eyes when he snatched it and stuffed it into his trousers), two cans of tinned salmon, a dented pot he'd been given when assigned the job of master cook for his company, and the extra pair of socks he'd darned just before the Mansfield battle.

#

In the room below Oliver's, old man Johnson and his wife were snoring. The sounds were nearly as loud as the wind outside. It was curious that they were able to sleep through each other's snorts and rumbles. Oliver wanted to stomp on the floor to make them shut up, but he knew the effort would be wasted and only make him more tired, more angry.

Licking his dried lips, he stared at his socked feet. The socks had holes in them, but he didn't have the energy to mend them. They were threadbare, ready for the dust bin, yet they were the one pair he'd been able to keep in Andersonville prison. The ones the Raiders hadn't stolen. They were the ones he'd worn the day of his release seven months earlier, the ones he'd worn on his long trip back North.

Not a journey home to his mother and father in Ohio, oh, no, but one to Philadelphia, following the butcher Doctor Marcus Calhoun. Calhoun, who had served in the Army of the Confederacy on behalf of his Georgian family but when the war ended, had relocated to Philadelphia.

"Maybe you left Andersonville, Doctor Calhoun," Oliver swore each night before he fell asleep in his little boarding house room, "but you cannot leave behind what you've done. What I've done. I will seek you out, find you, and we will both pay."

Oliver put his face in his hands but didn't weep. Weeping was worthless, and his tears had dried up many months ago.

#

The first week in the prison had ground down into the second and a third, then April into May and May into June, more hot, humid, and foul with the passage of time. On the battlefield, Oliver had seen men bleed out in minutes and succumb to infection or disease in a matter of days. He'd seen men spent and suffering from not enough rations. But he had no idea how quickly a man could become an unrecognizable creature from intentional starvation and dehydration. He watched as Richard began to fade away from fear and fouled water. And Oliver himself, who had been a stouter young man at the beginning, was soon able to wrap his fingers around his wrist, and he wore his belt at the tightest notch so as not to lose his pants around his ankles.

The armed Confederate guards, high in their pigeon roosts, took sport in watching some of their imprisoned enemies devolve from robust, honorable men to thieving gangs who threatened and beat one another to steal clots of molded corn pone and tattered scraps of blankets while others become shambling, disoriented, stinking ghouls whose ribs and hipbones pressed against paper-thin flesh. Sometimes Oliver could hear the guards laughing high up along the wall, and the sound was that of crows waiting to pick away at carrion. Sometimes Oliver dreamed he had a fine hunting rifle, like the one he'd owned as a boy back home, and one by one picked the guards out of their roosts to the cheers of the other prisoners. When he awoke from these dreams he cursed and spit that they were not real.

Twice a week two guards and a prison doctor condescended to walk out among the prisoners, collecting those they would put into their ox-drawn wagon and take to the prison hospital outside the stockade. How they made their selections was a mystery. They might scoop up a few living skeletons and several men with severe stomach pains or festering sores, yet not come back for others as bad or worse. Ambulatory prisoners, some with shoes and some barefooted in the muck, upon seeing guards and the physician in their midst, would swarm the wagon with demands. Hands would reach up and out, clutching, begging.

"The Raiders stole three days of my ration, sir! I'm going to perish like the others!"

"We got to get some fresh water, sir! My tongue's swelling up like a catfish and I can hardly swallow!"

"Please, doctor!"

"Listen sir!"

"Have pity!"

"Shoot me, sir!"

"Put m' buddy out of his misery, sir! He's in so much agony!"

And thus life in the prison dragged on.

It was a fateful day when Oliver bargained for help for Richard. It was mid-June. Richard was lethargic and only able to hold down a few bites of the corn pone that Oliver tried to feed him. He could only lie silently in the stinking tent by the swamp, waiting to die, his chest heaving, flies rimming his eyes.

Oliver pulled himself to his feet and went after the wagon. He grabbed the ox's harness and pulled the animal to a halt.

"Sirs!" he called. "My friend needs the hospital real bad."

One guard shoved Oliver back. "Move on!" he snarled. "Can't help all you damn Yankees, now get out of our way."

"My friend is quite sick!"

"Aren't you all?" asked the doctor.

"Please."

"Move away or I'll knock you away," said the first guard.

"Or shoot you down," said the second guard.

"I..." began Oliver. The lie then tumbled out of his mouth with ease. "I'm trained in medicine. Take Richard to the hospital and I'll come, too. I'm quite skilled. I can help there, when I'm of no help here in the compound."

The doctor, a tall and imposing man with black eyes and a white beard, took a step toward Oliver. "You're a doctor, you say?"

"I know a great deal about treating the sick and injured."

"Push him back," said the first guard. "He's wasting our time."

But the doctor rubbed his beard and said, "We could use another pair of trained hands."

"Doctor Calhoun!" complained the second guard.

The doctor considered Oliver. "What's your name, son?"

"O'Donnell."

"From New York?"

"Ohio."

"Got an aunt and uncle in Ohio."

"It's pretty land, Ohio," said Oliver.

The doctor tapped his front teeth with a finger, and then looked at the guards. "We'll take him with us. Never hurts to have an extra pair of hands that know what they're doing."

"But you must take my friend, Richard, too. That's the bargain."

One guard stepped up and slapped Richard so hard he fell back into the mud. "You don't dare bargain with us!"

"Let him be," said Doctor Calhoun. "Get up, boy. Where's your friend? We'll put him in the wagon with the others."

And so it was that Richard and Oliver left the main stockade and went to the hospital. Where Richard died. Where the nightmare to Oliver's nightmares began.

#

It wasn't long before Doctor Calhoun realized that Oliver had no medical training. He watched Oliver carefully with pursed lips and an arched brow, though he said nothing. Oliver had little choice but to continue the ruse, observing and imitating the actions of the doctors and assistants as best he could.

The hospital sat in a small field just south of the stockade, and consisted of numerous tents. Four tents formed "wards" in which men of various conditions were tended. Oliver had been assigned to the ward of the dying. No hope for these men, who had been transferred from other wards to get them out of the way and clear spaces for more patients. The staff in the dying ward was limited and they feigned at care, cleaning up the fluids that leaked from boils and festering wounds, patting down foreheads with damp rags, though offering no food and very little water to drink. There were no bandages for these men; in fact, there were few bandages for anyone in the hospital, and so to tend wounds of those who had no chance of recovery was considered wasteful. The dying men's grave injuries were covered with flies and swarmed with maggots. These men moaned and writhed on their blankets on the ground, begging for someone to help them. When no one was watching, Oliver poured turpentine into their wounds, which caused them to hiss and clench their teeth, but it killed the wriggling worms for the time being.

Doctor Calhoun, one of the hospital's five surgeons, always visited the death ward as the last stop before he retired for the day. The old physician seemed to be intrigued by the dyings' mental states as much as their physical conditions. He would hold a man's hand and ask, "How's the pain, son?" And then, looking more closely into the man's eyes, he'd whisper, "Are you afraid to die? Do you imagine you're heading to Hell as reward for those you killed in battle?"

Oliver felt his stomach twist whenever he saw the doctor coming, but kept on dabbing, wiping, patting.

Richard was placed in the ward for those with dysentery. Oliver hoped his placement meant Richard might recover, but he was dead in three days. He never made it as far as the dying ward. Oliver grieved mightily, weeping into his blanket in the hospital assistants' tent at night, and thought in moments of dark weakness that he would prefer to up and die, himself. War was hell. Andersonville was Hell's hell.

One afternoon, as Oliver helped another assistant carry one of the dead out to the road where it and other corpses would be collected by mule-team wagons, hauled away, and buried in mass graves, Doctor Calhoun grabbed him by the elbow.

"Let's talk, boy," the doctor said.

Oliver cringed and dropped the dead man's legs. Surely it was time now that Calhoun would tell him he knew about his lie and would send him back to the stockade to face a dire punishment. Whipping perhaps. Maybe even hanging.

"Go on," Calhoun said to the other assistant. "This dead fellow doesn't weigh what a baby weighs. You can get him to the road on your own."

The assistant nodded glumly and dragged the body off.

Oliver looked at the doctor, at the deep-set, unreadable eyes. "What do you want?"

"In my tent, then we'll talk."

The doctor shared a large tent with the other physicians, who were currently out and about in the wards. Calhoun ushered Oliver into the mildewed shadows and pointed to a stool.

Oliver obediently sat.

Calhoun packed and lit a pipe. "So you lied to me, didn't you, boy?" he asked. He was smiling a most bizarre, raptor-like smile.

"You know that. Why ask me?"

"How did you feel when you lied? Did you feel brave and compassionate, trading the truth for your friend, Richard?"

"I..." Oliver frowned. He could think of no man he hated more than Doctor Calhoun, but the man held all the power here. "Yes, I did. Of course I did."

"I see." Calhoun nodded, frowned, crossed his arms. "And then Richard died. Did you feel betrayed?"

"I felt he was gone."

"Answer my question. Did you feel betrayed by Richard?"

"No."

"Did you feel betrayed by God?"

"I am too tired to feel betrayed by anything or anyone."

"Yes, all right, that makes sense." The doctor nodded again, then said, "I could kill you for lying, you know."

"I know."

"I asked about you over in the stockade. I talked to some of your fellows in their campsite by the swamp."

Oliver waited.

"They told me you were a cook for their company."

"Yes."

"And that you were a cook back in Ohio."

"A cook of sorts."

"You worked in a canning factory, they said."

"In Cleveland. For a year or so."

"Indeed." Calhoun's lip twitched. He scratched at his beard thoughtfully. "What did the factory can?"

"Beef."

"And you cooked the beef?"

Oliver stared out through the open tent flap. It had begun to rain, a steaming, foggy rain. The ox-drawn guard wagon pulled up to the main hospital tent with its load of the sick. He wondered if any of them were from his company. Samuel. Winston. George. He looked away, not wanting to know.

"I asked you a question. You cooked the beef?"

"Yes, of course," said Oliver. "Why?"

Doctor Calhoun said, "Come with me."

#

He woke with a start in his little cane chair near the window. The wind was still howling but the night was giving way to dawn, with faint sunlight bleeding onto the floor. Oliver wiped the crust from his eyes and pushed upward. His back ached, and his legs. They had ever since the war, ever since Andersonville, in spite of his young age. Torment and bad food and guilt will do that to a man.

Tugging on his trousers, shirt, suspenders, and shoes, and grabbing his jacket from the doorknob, Oliver made his way down the stairs to the first floor where Mrs. Warren was setting out the dishes for breakfast in the dining room.

"G'mornin', Mr. O'Donnell," she said. "Up early, I see."

Oliver nodded and slipped into his jacket.

"Joining us for breakfast, I trust?"

"No, ma'am, I'm not hungry."

Mrs. Warren put her hands on her ample hips. "Now, I'm not your mother but you must eat. You're little more than skin and bones."

Oliver buttoned his jacket.

"Molly and I are cooking eggs and potatoes, some bacon and some fine tinned meats."

Oliver knew she hadn't said tinned meats but she might have. She could have. His jaw tightened. "I'm going out, Mrs. Warren."

"Are you quite sure?"

"I'm sure."

He left the boarding house, heading west toward Locust Street.

#

Doctor Calhoun gave Oliver his own small cook tent, back and away from all the other tents of the hospital, deep in the pine trees. The doctor used his authority to tell the other staff member that it was his own private tent and no one was to bother it under any circumstances. The doctors and assistants assumed Calhoun would use it for trysts with local and willing ladies, so left well enough alone. Oliver was also given a large cauldron, salts and spices, and implements for preparing meats for canning.

"My brother has a canning factory in Macon," Calhoun told Oliver. "Meat's scarce in the Confederacy, you probably know. And tinned meats can last more than a year."

Oliver gazed at the little tent, the cauldron in the newly dug pit, and the tools placed out on a crude wooden bench.

"You will live here in this little tent, and you will work here," said Calhoun. "I'll get the unprepared meat to you, and you will prepare it. Then I will package it and send it to my brother."

Oliver frowned, fearing what he was hearing.

"Oh, not the truly diseased, of course," said Calhoun. "But the best bits and cuts that can be salvaged."

Dear God! I can't do this. I won't do this!

Calhoun smiled and patted Oliver on the back. "You look a bit reluctant."

Oliver couldn't speak.

"If you refuse, you'll hang."

Oliver stared at the cauldron then stared at Doctor Calhoun.

"How does it make you feel?" asked the doctor. "Are you conflicted? Are you shaking, trembling at the thought?"

Oliver said nothing.

"You'll do it."

Oliver bit the inside of his cheek until it bled. "I'll do it."

#

Doctor Marcus Calhoun had moved to Philadelphia easily. Though a Southerner, he had connections in the big city and had told Oliver that his loyalties lay mainly with himself. The man had found a house and opened a practice, which appeared to be doing fairly well.

Andersonville prison was liberated by the victorious Union and closed in May, a month following Lee's surrender to Grant. Some of the prisoners who were still alive were eager to testify against prison commandant Henry Wirz at a military tribunal. Wirz was found guilty and hanged November 10th. Oliver had no desire to testify against the commandant, though. His focus was Calhoun.

It took Oliver five months to make his way from Georgia to Pennsylvania, stealing, lying, and cheating to gain the money and clothing he needed. In Philadelphia, he secured a room in Mrs. Warren's boarding house and a job on the docks then went about searching for the doctor.

At last he located Calhoun's tidy brick house at the corner of Locust and Seventh Streets, and in the early mornings he watched it from the shadows, noting the man's comings and goings. Calhoun lived with another man, a cousin, perhaps, and spent a lot of time in the house. Patients came to him, though on occasion Oliver saw him leave by carriage with his black bag in hand.

He needed a firearm, something to hide in his coat, something Calhoun wouldn't see until the last moment. And so he put as much of his earnings away, hiding the money in a dresser drawer, counting it each night.

And then he had enough for a Colt revolver. A weapon he knew well.

"At least take a biscuit with you!" Mrs. Warren called from the boarding house door as Oliver strolled off down the street. "Mr. O'Donnell?"

He pretended not to hear her. He had no appetite for breakfast nor for what he was doing to do. Though it had to be done.

#

Arms. Legs. Slices of thighs and buttocks.

He cooked them all in the cauldron over pine wood fires, boiling them down, seasoning them as best he remembered how to, letting them cool then wrapping the meat in bundles. He slept little and thought even less.

Feet, shoulders, bellies.

Once Calhoun brought over a head with the rest of the parts. When the doctor was gone, Oliver flung the head far into the pine trees. That night he dreamed the head was making its way back to his little tent with its accusatory grin and blood-stained teeth.

The day after the head was sent, Calhoun stopped by to watch Oliver work, stirring, straining the meats.

"What did you think when you saw the head?"

"Nothing."

"No, how did it make you feel? Was it someone you knew?"

"No."

"Were you upset? Did you feel like an animal?"

"I am what I am."

"Are you an animal, Oliver?"

Oliver scraped a layer of grease from the top of the cauldron. In the corners of his vision, in the shadows of the pines, skeletons jeered and pointed at him. "I am what I am. Go away, let me work."

#

He hid across the street from Doctor Calhoun's house until twilight, crouching among the hedges of a well-tended garden. He had not seen the doctor leave, only his companion, but Oliver would not go up to the house and knock. The confrontation had to be in the open; Calhoun could not have an escape into his home.

Late-season flies hovered around him, knocking into his face, crawling on his sleeves. He thought of the faces of the men in the stockade, trying feebly to brush the flies away, and of the men in the dying ward, no longer able to move a hand against the insects. He shut his eyes for a moment, and saw flies dancing greedily in the oily air above the cauldron in the pines as the meat bubbled and turned.

Damn you to the worst of Hell, Doctor Calhoun!

He opened his eyes as a wagon rumbled past, and though it was filled with pumpkins, Oliver saw heads with eyes wide, gazing at him, glaring at him, as their brittle lips attempted to speak.

Then – there. The door to the house opened and Doctor Calhoun stepped out onto the stoop, dressed in a nice overcoat and top hat. Oliver clambered from the hedges and darted across the street, one hand inside his jacket, fingers around the revolver.

"Doctor Calhoun, sir!"

Calhoun looked over his shoulder at Oliver. There was no recognition in his expression.

"Go away, boy, I don't give to beggars."

Oliver stopped two feet from the man. He stared, struggling to breathe, his hands slick with sweat as the memories of Andersonville, one upon another upon another, slammed into his mind.

"You," he managed, "you don't remember me."

The doctor sneered. "Should I remember you?"

"You must remember."

The doctor tipped his head, tugged at his chin, and then said cheerfully, "Ah, wait! Yes! Fate has reunited us after all these many months. Andersonville Prison. You are Mr. O'Donnell, if I live and breathe."

"I found you."

"Was I lost?"

"We have business."

"Do we? I don't think so."

"Unfinished business."'

"War is over, boy. War is in the past."

"It's not in the past. It's never in the past. The war is over but the torment isn't! It never leaves me. I'm never free of it." Oliver pulled the revolver from his coat and pointed it at Calhoun. It shook wildly in his hand. "The battles themselves were dreadful, yes, and the Andersonville stockade immoral beyond imagining. Yet worse still, worst of all, is what you forced me to do! I shall never free of that. It has followed me, horrified me, ever since. I am destroyed because of you!"

Calhoun grinned. "I didn't make you do anything. You did it of your own free will."

"You would have had me hanged!"

"No, I would not have."

"What…no?"

"I'm not a killer, boy. I'm a healer."

"Healer? You are a devil!"

Calhoun crossed his arms and stepped closer to Oliver. He leaned in, seeming oblivious to the wavering revolver. "Tell me, then. You say you are still in agony over what you did for me? Are there nightmares?"

"Of course!"

"They've not abated over all these months?"

"They've grown worse! Ghosts! Phantoms! I dream of tins of foods splitting open, and of hands grabbing me and pulling me into inescapable maws! I dream of the screams of the men who have been consumed! I dream of those hapless souls we reduced to meals for unknowing hundreds, maybe thousands! The terror does not end, Doctor!"

"Yes!" The doctor clapped his hands. "I shall write this in my study! Such twist of fate we've found each other."

"No twist of fate." Oliver panted, swallowed hard. "I've hunted you. I will kill you for what you've done, and then myself. You and your brother have tinned the flesh of helpless prisoners for profit. You made me part of your hideous scheme!"

"So, young friend, do you fear eternal fires of Hell for what you've done?"

"What? Yes, of course!"

"Are you able to work? Do you have appetite? Can you eat beef? What is it like to be so troubled?"

"Shut up!" screamed Oliver. "Why are you asking me such questions? What difference does it make in light of our mortal sin?"

Calhoun made a *tsking* sound and then said, "We've done nothing, boy. There is no canning factory. I haven't even got a brother."

Oliver stared.

"The raw meats I sent you to cook were just parts of bodies bound for burial. I wanted to know what would become of the mind of a man if he thought he was committing something unforgiveable in the sight of God. Ah, and you were so dutiful. What a fine job you did with the meat. It smelled almost good enough to eat, but heavens! That would be ghastly, indeed. I learned that a man might become numbed to such an act, as you seemed to have. But now, now I see that the numbness was only temporary, and the anguish lingers in the mind. It bores in and remains much like a beetle in the soft wood of a pine tree."

Oliver stared. "You did that to me? I was an experiment?"

Calhoun said, "I will add this to my journals. Thank you, Mr. O'Donnell. I'm very glad you found me and told me of your troubles. But now you can let your worries go, as you know the truth." He turned and strode off through the darkness of approaching night, chuckling cheerfully.

Oliver stared. The revolver slipped from his hand.

He followed it, down to his knees.

All was Hell.

Darla and Gina Try to Keep Out of Debt

"My best calculation is that we can make it another two months on our savings and your income," said Gina. "But after that, we have only what you make, and honey, that isn't going to be enough."

Darla sat across from Gina at the kitchen table, one hand tucked beneath the soft skin of her chin, the other clutching the coffee cup next to her plate of half-eaten eggs. Dust drifted on the Sunday morning sunlight. Through the open kitchen window, the sounds of neighbors mowing filled the air.

"Darla?"

Darla focused on her wife across the table. Gina was a slender, athletic woman of sixty-one, her short hair salt and pepper, her eyes blue chips in a taut and serious face. "What?"

"We're running out of money."

"I heard."

"And I haven't sold a painting in close to a year," said Gina. "What you make at the insurance company pays more than half but not all."

"I know."

"It looks like I'll have to get a job somewhere, then, close up my studio, just forget being an artist. I was afraid that would happen someday. That day is now, sadly."

Darla sighed. "Don't say that, Gina. You are a fantastic artist."

"People don't love my work anymore. Nobody's buying squat." Gina glared down at the food on own breakfast plate. She hadn't eaten a single bite. That was how she got when she was stressed, frustrated, or both.

"Things could change," said Darla.

"Don't be naïve."

"I'm not."

"Maybe I can hand out carts at the store," said Gina, though her expression told Darla that she'd rather be dead. "Or I can take orders for burgers at the joint down the street. Old ladies do that all the time."

Darla took a sip of coffee, now lukewarm. "Gina, don't. We've had tight times before and always made it through somehow."

Gina pushed back in her chair and stood up. She spun away toward the window, her hands on her hips. "Right." Her voice was dark and tight. "Right, Darla. And that was back when my artwork was in vogue. You know, vogue, like the old Madonna song?" Gina made little boxes around her face and then let her hands drop to her sides.

"I can ask for a raise," Darla offered.

"An extra dollar an hour isn't going to help us that much, don't you know that?"

Darla knew that, she just didn't know what else to offer at the moment.

It was going to be a long day.

When the women came back together at noon for lunch, Darla could barely contain herself. "I have a great idea, and don't say no before you have a chance to think it through."

Gina was still on edge; she'd spent the rest of the morning upstairs in her studio, banging around, maybe painting but probably not. She settled down with her deviled ham sandwich and carrot sticks and sent a look across the table at Gina that said, "Okay, impress me."

"Honey, this will sound odd at first," Darla began. "But here me out first."

"What?"

"You'll listen. You'll count to sixty before saying anything?"

Gina's face softened a little. In spite of her often-curmudgeonly ways, she did love Gina, and had for the last twenty-three years. "All right. What?"

Darla said, "You remember that movie, *The Full Monty*?"

Gina's eyes widened. "I'm not stripping!"

"No, not that. But you remember that movie? And the movie about the women who posed nude over in England for a calendar, so they could raise money? I think it was called *Calendar Girls* or something like that."

"I'm not posing nude, either!"

"No, Gina. Not that, either." Darla picked up her own sandwich and looked at Gina from over the bread. "You ready to hear it?"

Gina nodded, barely.

"I say we do a little prostituting here at home, real quiet like. Now count to sixty, you promised."

Gina's mouth fell open. Thank goodness she'd swallowed her bite of deviled ham, or it would have been rather nasty. Her finger began to tap on the tabletop, fast, too fast to be actual seconds, but at least she was counting. In about thirty seconds she had reached sixty. Then she exploded.

"You have to be out of your mind! Prostitutes? First of all, neither of us cares for men, in case you hadn't figured that out, Second of all, it's illegal!"

There was more to come. Darla just had to wait it out.

"Third, how on Earth would we advertise? Fourth, it's dangerous. Hookers get killed all the time by crazed johns or at the very least they get arrested. You watch as much CSI as I do, Darla."

Darla nodded.

"Fifth, we aren't exactly the type of women men are looking for," said Gina. "We're far from young, and far from pretty."

"You're pretty," said Darla.

Gina made a mouth noise that sounded like, "humph." Then she said, "Well, thank you, dear, but you know what I mean."

"I know what you mean."

"And for some bizarre, insane reason you think this could work?"

Ah, she was coming around. "Gina, this can be as discreet as we need it to be. We can put an ad in the local paper and see what happens. The ad won't say, 'Old women to have sex for money.' It can be veiled, like 'Women in their prime available to assist those in need of special care.' Something along those lines."

"That's too discreet," said Gina. She took another bite of sandwich and looked at Darla with narrowed lids. "Who would know what we were really advertising?"

"I think there are enough men out there who like older women and want to have sex with them to read between the lines."

Gina winced but Darla kept on.

"We won't include our phone number or e-mail addresses. Just our home address."

Gina shook her head. "You want folks to just stop on by for a quickie without making an appointment first?"

"Not exactly like that. I figure those who are curious will come by. If they're real customers, and they seem safe, we'll let them in and do, well, whatever it takes. Get the money and send them home. If people come by who seem dangerous, or like they're the law, we'll tell them we're seamstresses and our special care is making comfortable lounge wear for those just out of the hospital or in nursing homes. We'll set my sewing machine in the front room, I'll buy some yardage of cheap flannel, drape it around, so it looks real."

Gina look a long breath, held it, let it out. For the next few minuets she silently chewed her way through the rest of her sandwich without so much as glancing at Darla. Instead, she stared at the calculator she'd left in the middle of the table. Darla could read the mental mathematics going on behind the blue eyes.

Then, still without looking across the table: "How much do women like that charge per hour?"

"It varies."

"How do you know?"

"I've looked it up online. It can also be priced for the act rather than the time."

"The *act*?" Gina looked from the calculator to Darla.

"You know, a hand job gets a certain amount. A regular ride – which means sex – a certain amount. Dressing up in costumes, maybe, or pretending to be a cat or bunny rabbit would bring in another amount."

"Ugh," said Gina. "I'm not sure I can do this."

"You've done lots of unpleasant things in life, Gina. You've mucked stables and scrubbed toilets. When I had the flu last fall you cleaned up after me for more than a week. And that was nasty, you can't deny it."

"Well…"

"And I saw your face when you thought about handing out grocery carts or taking orders for fast food hot apple pies. Is one really much worse than the other? And my idea would pay a lot more."

"How much?"

"Okay." Darla hopped up, went into the living room, and brought back a legal pad on which she had scratched down suggested fees. "This is what I've figured out, though please, I'd love some input."

Gina's lip hitched up, down.

"First of all, no blow jobs. I'm not risking putting some diseased…you know…in my mouth for any amount of money. I'd rather die."

"I agree one hundred percent."

"I think we should offer hand jobs, with some nice almond scented lotion, for one hundred dollars. We do it right, the guy could come in, what ten minutes?"

"I don't know how long it takes a guy to come."

"Let's say ten minutes. That's one hundred dollars for ten minutes. An hour of that, we've made six hundred dollars!"

"I'm not jacking off six men in a row."

"No, well, but you know what I mean. I'm just saying it's a good rate."

"What else, Darla?"

"Straight sex, face to face, three hundred dollars, minimum. I figure that might take longer, maybe a half hour. But still, there's our six hundred dollar an hour rate. Do you see?"

Gina rolled her eyes but waved one hand that suggested, "Go on."

"We can roll play. Some men like that."

"Some women like that."

"Just listen, okay? Let's say we come up with five or six costumes. School girl..."

"Ha!"

"...nurse, French maid, teacher, waitress. That kind of thing. I can sew them, cheap. A roll play episode with one of us, ending in ordinary face-to-face sex, would be five hundred dollars. If we are both involved, the fee is seven hundred dollars."

"Why not a thousand for both?"

"We should offer some kind of price reduced incentive."

Gina ran her fingers through her short hair and closed her eyes. "This makes my head hurt."

"I know, Honey," said Darla. "But a couple months of this and we should have a tidy sum tucked away in savings. Enough to get by until your paintings start to sell again."

"If ever."

"But this will give us the time and income so you can try, right?"

There was a long pause. Long enough for Darla to watch through the window as the women next door started up her riding mower, drove it the length of the yard, turned it off and went back inside, probably for a canned soda for her mower's drink holder.

Then Gina began, "But what if...?"

"We can require condoms."

"And if they want us to do something we don't want to do?"

"We can come up with a compromise."

"And if they stink?"

"We can bathe them for an additional hundred. We can use the guest room in the back. There's everything we need. A bed, only one window, the small bathroom with the shower stall."

Gina rubbed the tip of her nose. "So you've got all the bases covered?"

Darla grinned. "Except for the costumes, and I'll get on those this afternoon!"

It took a full week for Darla to sew several identical costumes – the nurse, the maid, and the waitress – for both herself and Gina. Gina's costumes were small; Darla's fluctuated between a size 16 and 18, depending on the patterns, which she bought, along with some lovely pieces of pink, green, and striped flannel down at the fabric store. And even though the pattern didn't offer it, Darla used her own imagination to sew up two perky, lacy white caps to go with the waitress get-up, which had only included a dress and an apron.

Then, Darla composed the ad: "Lovely middle-aged ladies prepared to help make the lives of uncomfortable men more comfortable, 6-9 p.m. weeknights, 9-7 p.m. weekends. 1837 Madison Street. Come by to set up an appointment."

Gina balked at this initially, thought the wording might suggest too much, but then agreed the "sewing post-hospital clothing" could fit as a definition as to what was being offered if someone pushed the point. However, she questioned why Darla had limited the invitation to men.

"I've researched the business," Darla explained. "Men by far are the biggest customers. As a salesperson, I'm of the belief that we should target our most likely clients initially."

It seemed to please Gina that women weren't as prone to paying for sex as their male counterparts.

The following Wednesday the classified ad appeared in the local newspaper, both the online and the print editions. Darla was dismayed that someone had stuck the ad it in the miscellaneous section rather than the services as she had requested, but Gina said it probably didn't matter.

No one stopped by Thursday. No one stopped by Friday. On Saturday, the lady next door stopped by to ask what the ad in the paper was all about, that her husband had hemorrhoids and if they had something she could buy, some herbal medicines or something homeopathic that he hadn't tried that might actually work, it would make his life easier and in turn make her life a hell of a lot easier. Darla smiled apologetically and pointed to the flannel cloth draped over the back of her sewing chair. "Sorry," she said. "We're making clothes for bed ridden or homebound folks."

"But only men?" the woman asked.

"Ah, well," said Darla. "I got a great deal on men's patterns, you see."

"Oh, all right," said the neighbor. She left, shoulders down, clearly disappointed.

Sunday morning no one showed up. Late Sunday afternoon, as Darla was putting together a batch of vegetable soup for the week and Gina was upstairs, trying to paint, there was a knock on the door. Darla rinsed her hands and went out to the front, expecting nothing more than some kid with a brochure trying to collect pledges for some kind of walk-a-thon-or-other. The ad had been in the paper for five days; both Darla and Gina had anticipated some business by then. But there had been nothing.

Until this man.

It was hard to judge his age, somewhere between forty and fifty, with a pinched red face, a body as bloated as a Macy's Thanksgiving Day Parade balloon, and tiny little feet that didn't seem as if they could keep him upright in a strong wind. He wore an enormous red t-shirt and a pair of gray sweatpants. His hands were clasped before him as if he was ready to apologize for anything, everything he might do wrong.

Darla's fist thought was, This guy is selling something we don't want. Her second thought, which popped into her head with incredulity, was, *Did this man actually read our ad?*

"May I help you?" asked Darla without opening the screen door.

"I'm uncomfortable," the man said, and then his eyes squished up in embarrassment, as if the words on the air actually startled him.

Darla collected her wits, and tried to project the professional she imagined she was. "You saw our ad?"

"Yes."

"And do you have a specific need, Mr...?"

"Um. Can we just make it Smith?"

"Absolutely."

"Can I come in first? I don't like standing out here."

Darla opened the door, and Mr. Smith squeezed past her into the living room, a scent of Old Spice and chicken chow mein in his wake. He looked at the sewing machine, and the cloth, and confusion flickered over his face. Perhaps he was wondering if he'd misread the ad, if the ladies in question only sewed comfortable clothes for uncomfortable men.

"Gina!" Darla called upstairs without looking away from Mr. Smith. "We have company!"

Gina could be heard thumping around upstairs, and then her studio door opened. "What?"

"We have company! Mr. Smith read our ad!"

Darla couldn't hear it but she knew Gina had cursed at that. The air had shifted inside the little house. Here they were, ready to tackle their first client. It was real, it was happening. And both of them were nervous as hell.

"Would you like some tea?" offered Darla.

Mr. Smith scratched at a spot beside his lower lip. He didn't look dangerous; he didn't look diseased, whatever that really looked like. He wasn't the law; didn't police officers have to maintain some semblance of fitness? Just a little?

"Tea? Oh, no thanks, I don't drink tea."

"Soda?"

"What kind?"

"Well, we buy the store brand cola..."

"Oh, then, no thanks. I like Dr. Pepper."

Gina tromped down the steps. She eyed Mr. Smith and he eyed her. She smiled with a tense jaw, held out her hand, and took Mr. Smith's pudgy fingers in her own. "Welcome. How can we help you?"

"I saw your ad...," Mr. Smith trailed.

Gina went to the front door and closed it, shutting off the stream of sunlight and heat pouring in through the screen. Mr. Smith glanced back as if he had just been trapped. "Don't worry, we'll turn on the air-conditioning so it doesn't get so hot in here," said Gina. "But it's best we keep the door shut, don't you think?"

Mr. Smith nodded weakly. Then said, "How much do you charge? I don't have a lot."

Gina cast Darla a look of dismay. Then she forced a smile again. "Well, we do have our fees. I suggest you hear what we have to offer before we talk any further."

Darla jumped in, "So, what do you do for a living, Mr. Smith?"

"I'm between jobs," said Mr. Smith.

Gina's look of dismay returned, and lingered a bit longer. "Well," she said, "we have comfort at several levels, ranging from one hundred dollars to a thousand, with other levels in between. But we assure you, whichever you choose will be worth your hard-earned..."

"Not really earned, Gina," said Darla.

"Your cash, wherever you get it."

"I have seventy-five dollars," said Mr. Smith, fumbling at the pocket of his sweatpants. The pants were stretched so tightly across his bulging belly that he had to lean back to wriggle his fingers inside. He pulled out a couple crinkled twenties, a ten, and some ones. "On that TV show, *Cops*, guys get stuff done for just twenty-five. I thought I would have enough for three sessions, maybe spread out over next week?"

Gina said, "I'm going to get some coffee, Darla. Could you handle this?" The voice was steady but there was steam just below the surface. She was getting ready to blow.

As Gina went back to the kitchen, Darla rubbed her neck and said, "Listen, Mr. Smith, the women on Cops are whores, drugged-out hookers. I'm sure you are aware of that. We, on the other hand, are dignified, intelligent, mature women. You get what you pay for. Trash or treasure. And besides, there are no other services like this anywhere else in town. You'd have to go all the way to the city and that's more than an hour drive."

"Well." Mr. Smith shuffled his feet. He looked at the floor and then at the dollars in his hand. "What can I get for the whole seventy five?"

Darla was getting ready to say, "Clearly you didn't hear me, our lowest fee is one hundred," but then again, a john in the house was worth two in someone else's bush, so she decided, "Okay, Mr. Smith. We can give you a lovely hand job for that."

"Is that all?" Mr. Smith's face drew up and his lip dropped down. Damn, but Darla hated pouters. She almost kicked him in the balls but that would end the deal.

She moved up close to Mr. Smith and put her hand on his crotch, or the basic area thereof. She could feel something she guessed was his penis beneath a roll of flesh, a small, crushed protuberance that could also have been a wad in his shorts.

Mr. Smith moved one leg aside to give her more room. He began to pant. Darla swallowed back her revulsion and rubbed at the knot of flesh between his legs.

Think of kneading dough, she told herself. *Nice, fresh dough to bake rolls for Gina and my dinner.*

Then she stopped, stepped back, and said, "How about it, Mr. Smith? Do we have your business?"

There were sweat beads already on his forehead, little greasy dots of wet. He said, "Yes, please. I'll pay. Don't stop."

Darla led the man to the back bedroom. She and Gina hadn't done much to the small space to make it look like a proper bordello, but the bed had a nice chenille bedspread, the braided rug had been newly shampooed, and scented bayberry candles Darla had bought last Christmas but hadn't used sat in pewter holders, awaiting the touch of a match. Gina's old lava lamp was nestled on the nightstand between a box of tissues and a vase with plastic purple irises. The straight-back chair had a brand new scarlet cushion.

Mr. Smith sat down on the bed, the box springs groaning beneath him. He kicked off his shoes, releasing a smell of old cheese into the room.

"Ah, hmm," said Darla as she watched him peel off his thin socks.

"We have a bathroom in here." She swept her hand toward the partially opened door. "Why don't you go wash up before we get started? Wash your feet, everything else. We've got washcloths laid out, and some lovely lavender soap."

"You do that for me," said Mr. Smith. "You wash me. Please? My mama used to wash me but she won't do it anymore." He struggled up from the bed then grappled at the elastic on his waistband, and shoved the sweatpants down to his knees. For a moment, the penis was visible, sticking out stiff and ready from beneath the white flesh. Then Mr. Smith fell back on the bed, unable to keep upright with his pants down. Out the door and across the hall, Darla could hear Gina's teakettle whistle. She wasn't going to come to the bedroom. She was going to let Darla take the maiden voyage.

"Your...mama?"

Mr. Smith nodded. He shuffled his legs up and down, working the pants down to the floor where he kicked them aside. Then, flat on his back, he licked his lips, balled his fat fingers together, and looked up at Darla with hideously hopefully eyes.

"My mama used to wash my pee-pee," said Mr. Smith in a voice suddenly pitched high and squeaky. "Wash my pee-pee, Mama. Rub it so it feels good."

Holy crap!

"Mama," whimpered the big, bare-assed man on the bed, "rub my pee-pee and make it feel good."

Darla looked at Mr. Smith, at the reddened penis poking up like a newborn prairie dog, and at the balled-up fists and the blubbery, expectant face. She took a breath, and another. Then another. Then, with shaking fingers, she pulled open the little drawer in the night table and took out a condom.

"What's that, Mama?" whined Mr. Smith.

"A condom. Safe sex, you know."

Mr. Smith's lower lip quivered and he pushed himself up on his elbow. "No condoms. Mama's don't make their baby boys use condoms."

"Well...dear...," said Darla as she tore open the packet. "This Mama does."

"No!"

"Shh, lay still." She grasped the little rubbery cap with her fingers and bent down, aiming it at the prairie dog. Suddenly, Mr. Smith roared upright on the bed, and he shoved Darla away. She landed on her butt on the floor.

"I said no condoms!" He rocked back and forth, trying to struggle to his feet. "Mamas don't do that, mamas like their baby boys' pee-pees just the way they are!"

"Gina!" cried Darla.

Mr. Smith made it off the bed, and he grabbed Darla's hair and pulled her head toward his penis. "Kiss it, Mama! Kiss it and make it better!"

Darla clawed at Mr. Smith's hands, twisting her head back and forth, feeling hunks of hair coming loose. The prairie dog loomed only inches away. She closed her eyes.

"Gina!"

And then there was a whooshing sound over her head, and a gasp, and a crash. More hair came out of her head by the roots with sparks of white-hot pain, but then the pressure was gone. Darla opened her eyes, and wiped the tears away to clear her vision.

Gina stood beside her, hands on hips, staring down at Mr. Smith. Mr. Smith lay squealing on the floor, the straight-back chair knocked to its side. The man's leg was broken, twisted as he'd tripped over the chair.

"Call 911!" screamed Mr. Smith, his eyes popping. "My leg! My leg!"

"You aren't telling us what to do, Mr. Smith," said Gina calmly. She looked at Darla, put out her hand to help her up. "You okay, Sweetie?"

"My head hurts."

"I'm sure it does."

"What are we going to do?" Darla rubbed her mouth anxiously.

"He's too fat for us to get him out of here. And if we call 911, we'll be found out, or at least there will be some serious questions!"

Gina sighed. Then she reached for the man's sweatpants and fished around in the pockets. There was a wallet in one of the back ones. She flipped it open, thumbed through, then said, "Mr. Smith, I see you're really Mr. Bradford Ellis."

"Call an ambulance!" screamed Mr. Bradford Ellis.

Gina held up a finger. "Now just wait a moment. Ellis. Ellis. I know that name. There is only one Ellis in town. And that would be the Margaret Ellis family, over on Crest Ridge Hill. The Margaret Ellis family that owns more than half of the businesses in the area, yes? The Margaret Ellis family that is richer than God. The Margaret Ellis family that wouldn't want a smudge on their lily white reputation. So, you're Margaret's little boy. Little man."

Mr. Bradford Ellis squirmed on the floor, too big and in too much pain to get up. "Call an ambulance right now!"

"Whatever," said Darla.

Gina stroked her chin. "I think we should call your Mama, Mr. Ellis, and have her come get you."

Mr. Bradford Ellis's wide eyes grew wider. "No! Don't you dare tell her! Ow! Ow!"

"Darla, please get the phone out of the kitchen."

Darla hurried for the phone and the phone book, and brought them back to Gina. Gina sat casually on the bed, looked up the Ellis number, and punched it in.

Then, "Hello, Mrs. Ellis? This is Gina Richards over on Monroe. No, I'm not selling anything, but...yes, that's right. Gina Richards, the painter.... Oh, really? That's wonderful. I'm so glad you've enjoyed my work, Mrs. Ellis. I hope to have some new works soon.... Yes, yes."

Mr. Ellis slammed one fist into his mouth so he wouldn't cry out, and slammed the other fist against the floor. His face was as red as a tomato from Gina's little garden.

"I did want to tell you that your son is here. He stopped by for a visit, you see and...Yes, you could say we're good friends. We've gotten to know each other fairly well recently." Then Gina went silent as she listened to Margaret Ellis on the line. Darla watched her face as it went from curious to thoughtful to triumphant. Then, "Well, then, certainly, we just might be able to figure something out along those lines, though I'll have to talk with my roommate. Could we call you back?...All right. Thank you, so much, Mrs. Ellis." Gina pushed the off button on the receiver.

"What? What did she say?" demanded Mr. Ellis.

Gina led Darla into the hallway and closed the back room door.

"Mrs. Ellis said she is very happy to hear that her son Braddie has some friends," said Gina. "She was very candid, said he'd been living with her his whole life and that she's tried her best to get him out into the world. Said her boy needed to grow up."

Darla wasn't sure where this was going. "And?"

"She said she wondered if we might consider letting him board with us for a while, so he can learn what it's like to live away from home."

"And?"

"I said we'd give it some thought."

"I don't understand."

Darla and Gina went into the kitchen. They poured themselves cups of tea and sat down at the table to sip and think. It didn't take long, actually. Room and board could be sixteen hundred a month. That would be reasonable enough for Mrs. Ellis not to get suspicious and enough money to cover what they needed and then some. They could keep Mr. Ellis comfy enough on the floor with some pillows and a bedpan. As bad as his leg was, he wouldn't be up and about for at least two months. They would let him call home once a week, under Darla and Gina's supervision, of course. They would have to keep him in food, to keep him fat and unable to get away, though they could go the cheap route. After all, there was the burger place down the street.

As Darla rinsed her teacup in the sink, she asked, "But when the leg is healed?"

Gina shrugged. "He might just break it again. Strikes me as the clumsy sort."

Darla nodded, smiled, and went back to chopping carrots and potatoes for the vegetable soup.

Whistling, Gina went upstairs to paint.

Don't Look at Me

Yeah, yeah, I know. I know I look like shit. But what do you expect? I've sat here in the tangled weeds at a far corner of Concrete City - a wholesale place that sells ornamental lawn decorations, birdbaths, angel and pig statues, and other pieces of so-called concrete art - for more than three years now. Here by the back fence where the property ends against a narrow portion of shoreline of an algae-crusted lake. Here amid the mosquitoes, snakes, spiders' webs, salamanders, and gobs of sticky goose poop. Here with the rest of the concrete outcasts. I disgust you, so don't look at me. Won't hurt my feelings a bit.

I got no legs, just feet peeking out from a ridiculous tunic. Little pudgy hands. No arms. No genitalia. No working eyes, so I can't see. A prissy, pointed hat with the tip chipped off, a hat that starlings find particularly perchable. If I had a real painted mouth, I could yell at them to get the hell off my head. But my mouth is just a slash in the concrete, which means I can't yell. Or speak. Or even hiss. And so I sit and wait here in the weeds. Wait with the other slightly irregular garden gnomes, elves, and fairies. More than likely no one will buy us. Shoppers prefer the new, perfectly-formed, brightly-colored concrete creatures out front of the warehouse, all lined up in rows for customers to inspect and admire.

Okay, let me clarify a few things for those who don't know. Things that are created in the shape of humans or near-humans have minds and we can think. Statuary. Puppets. Ventriloquist dummies. Dolls of all kinds – fashion dolls, action figures, sex dolls. And yes, garden gnomes like me. That creep you out? Get over it. It's your fault, anyway. You're the ones who made us. You are our gods. You fashion us out of concrete or marble or wood or plastic or stuffed cloth sacks and then you go and get weirded-out because there's more to us than you imagined there would be? Or hoped there would be? Grow up. Yeah, we think. And if we have properly painted mouths and eyes, we can also see and speak. You probably suspected that when you were a child. You probably forgot or denied that when you became an adult.

We know what's going on. We know what you're up to.

Rain and snow and sleet here in the far corner of Concrete City don't bother me. What bothers me most is the boredom. None of the others out here can see or speak, either. We're all plain, unpainted cast offs, "seconds," banished from the main part of the sales lot but not discarded. On a rare occasion some person will wander back here and pick one of us for a doorstop. We can't see it happening but can hear it. How can we hear if our ears aren't painted? You made us. You tell me.

Yesterday, I heard a little kid back in the weeds with us. A girl I think, with her fluttering fingers and her high-pitched voice. She talked to herself, prattled on as she moved around in the weeks. She picked me up, put me down. Picked me up, put me down. She left. Then she came back several hours alter and picked me up, put me down. She said, "I like you." Then she was gone again in a rustling of the dead grasses. She was alone, I think. I didn't hear any adults with her. Maybe she lives nearby and was just out playing.

I hear a storm on its way. Thunder. A sharp wind rustles the grasses and the water of the lake slaps the shoreline. I smell worm-scented air and I wait for a downpour. It doesn't come, and is hot again in just a few minutes.

Night comes. Then morning. The little girl is here again. This time she picks me up and holds me close to her chest. Her hands are small and soft. "I like you," she whispers into my ear. I wish I could see her. She seems frail but pretty.

And then off we go. I'm tucked under her arm and am carried – *jostle jostle jostle* – away from Concrete City, away from the smell of the lake and the hum of the mosquitoes. If I had a functional mouth I'd call, "Good-bye, suckers!" to the other outcasts in the weeds but I don't so I can't.

Five or so minutes later, a door is opened and we enter a cool place. I detect the sharp scents of burned eggs and cigarette smoke. The door is eased shut behind us. The girl tiptoes with me under her arm, up some stairs. Every other step creaks. I realize I'm stolen goods. Kind of exciting, to be honest. I'm not bored now. Little Miss What's-Her-Name has spirited me away without paying. How about that. I wonder if the owner of Concrete City will notice. If he'll even care.

I'm tossed onto a bed and I bounce, once. The little girl drops down beside me, picks me up with now sweaty hands and says so quietly I can barely hear her, "I'll keep you with my other friends. You'll like them." I don't know if I'll like them, but I don't have much choice, do I? The girl mutters something I can't hear and then I'm swept up and put onto a dusty shelf, squeezed in between some kind of plastic doll and something made out of wood. I hate to hell I can't see, but I can feel them. No personal space here, obviously.

Someone downstairs screams, "Connie! Get your lazy ass down here, now! I heard you goin' upstairs! Where the hell you been?"

So her name is Connie. And some rude as hell adult is yelling at her. I hear Connie take a sharp breath, hear her shoes slap the floor, hear her thump down the steps.

"Hey, Newbie," says a voice to my right. It's a gruff voice, deep, sounding like sandpaper against a stick.

Of course, I can't reply; I can only wait.

"Oh, yeah, no real mouth," says the voice. "We'll get Connie to take care of that. She steals her mother's lipstick when Mom is drunk. Likes to pretend she's an adult, likes to dream about being grown up and out of this shit hole.

Lipstick isn't permanent but it should do you for a while. Tastes like wax but beggars can't be choosers."

"As long as the old bitch doesn't catch her with the lipstick," came a voice from the left. It's another deep voice but smooth, slick. "Remember what happened when Connie was caught with her mom's cigarettes? Damn."

There was a loud, long silence then, as if they were remembering something most unpleasant. *So*, I figure, *the bitch is Mom. The screamer from downstairs.*

"Well, anyway, Newbie, my name is Bobby," says the voice on the right. "I'm a dummy, but don't ever call me that. Connie got me for her birthday last year. Her dad gave me to her, before he left for good. Bitch threatened to chop me up and throw me in the fireplace once when Connie wet the bed, but they don't have a fireplace. Mom's an idiot."

"Complete idiot," says the voice on the left.

Downstairs, more yelling. "Damn it, Connie! I told you never to look at me like that!" A loud slap. A whimper.

"Bitch," says Bobby.

"Bitch," says the voice on the left.

Bitch, I think.

Another long silence. I start to feel sleepy (yes, we sleep) and then Bobby says, "Hey, Newbie."

What?

"Here's my advice. Just ignore most of what you hear around here. Otherwise, you'll lose your mind."

The plastic doll on the left says, "Yeah. Bobby's right. Just know that we give Connie some joy in her life. Probably the only joy she has."

What's your name, doll? I wonder.

The doll says, "Oh, yeah, I'm Princess Polly. Just shut up about that, okay?"

Okay.

#

Connie comes back to her room much later, breathing hard, sniffling. It wakes me up. I hear her flop down on the bed and mutter into her pillow. Downstairs, a television has cut on and it's some kind of arguing and loud music. Seems

Mom can't get enough arguing, either hers or somebody else's.

Bitch.

After a while, Connie's sniffles and mumblings slow and stop. She gets up and pulls Princess Polly from the shelf and sings something so faint I can't pick out the words, but the melody is kinda nice. Then I hear Princess Polly say something to Connie. Connie replies, "Yeah, I still got some lipstick that Mama didn't find."

Princess Polly is put back on the shelf next to me. I hear Connie digging around, in a drawer I think. Then she is back, and she picks me up, spins me around, and sets me down on the bed beside her.

"You got to look nice," she says. "Here."

I feel a waxy substance spread on my lips. Well, on two thirds of my lips. My mouth twitches a bit. I can feel words forming, even though the right corner of my mouth is still dead.

"Thank you," I say, though it comes out more like "Hank you," what with my whole mouth not working and all.

Connie says, matter-of-factly, "Welcome. Now your eyes."

Something wet is streaked around my eye sockets. Connie says, "I messed up. Wait." She rubs the wet off and starts again. Round the sockets with some kind of tiny brush. Then, "Well, I guess it's okay."

I blink. Blurry, painful light bleeds into my eyes. I blink again and Connie comes into view.

I cringe.

She is perhaps eleven, maybe a little younger. She has thin brown hair and a thin sallow face. Bruises the shape of fingers are on her neck and there are scratches on her forehead. Her left eye is blackened.

"I see you," I manage.

"I know," says Connie. "Now I got to put you back. Mama said I better be down to fix supper before five o'clock. I'm going to fry some bologna."

"Okay." I don't know what else to say. I'd like to tell Connie to give her mother a swift kick in the ass for me, but I'm thinking that wouldn't be a good idea.

At least for now.

Connie puts me back on the shelf between Bobby, a one-armed garishly-colored ventriloquist dummy and Princess Polly, some kind of GI Joe doll dressed in Barbie clothes.

"Shut up," says Princess Polly, even before I can poke fun.

I can see Connie's whole room now. What I'd imagined as a pink and lavender fairyland is a tiny, colorless cell with an unmade bed, tattered throw rug, and filthy walls. A picture of puppies hangs at a tilt from a nail. The happiness of this room pretty much matches the happiness of the far, weedy back lot at Concrete City.

Connie sits on her bed and twists her hair around her fingers. She chews her lip. I can see that her fingernails are bitten down to stubs. Then her Mom screams and Connie is up and out of the door.

"Her Mom do all that to her?" I ask Bobby.

"Oh, you bet," says Bobby. "Bitch is crazy, hateful crazy. Blames Connie for everything that goes wrong in her life. Her alcoholism. Connie's dad up and leaving. The fact that she can't hold a job. Smacks Connie around, treats her like a slave."

"Damn."

"The Mom's the ultimate liar, too," says Princess Polly. "A master at it. Got a restraining order against Connie's dad, and the dad's the only good person ever in Connie's life."

"Fuck."

"Yep," says Princess Polly

"You got a name, Newbie?" asks Bobby.

"Guess not."

"Nobody ever owned you before, then? Where'd you come from?"

"Connie stole me from Concrete City."

"Yeah, Connie," says Princess Polly. "She steals stuff all the time. I think it fills gaps."

"Fills gaps," says Bobby. "So you're a psychiatrist now? Where'd you learn about filling gaps?"

"Hear bits and pieces on one of Mom's talk shows."

"Huh."

"Shut up."

"Hey, Newbie, I'm going to suggest Connie name you Pointy," says Bobby. "You got that stupid, chipped off pointy hat."

"I don't care what she names me," I say, and at that moment I really don't. I am thinking about Connie and the lying bitch downstairs and how something has to be done. While we puppets and dummies and dolls and gnomes can talk and see and hear and think, we can't walk. Nope. Even if we have feet and legs, they aren't taking us anywhere. I'd love to jump off the shelf with Bobby and Princess Polly, run downstairs, and stomp the shit out of the bitch.

But we can't.

Still. Something has to be done.

#

Connie comes back upstairs after she fixes supper and her mother screams that the bologna is rancid, there is grease all over the stove, and to quit looking at her. Connie crawls under her bed and I can hear her counting. I think she has stolen some coins from her mother. When she comes back out, I see that yes, there are coins in her hand, some sweaty dimes, quarters. She puts them into a jar and hides the jar in a dresser drawer, under socks and underwear.

"Connie," I say. Stupid lips, only two-thirds working. I say it louder. "Connie!"

Connie looks over at the shelf, her head tipped in curiosity, her stringy hair cupping her cheek. She comes over and leans in. The blackened bruise around her eye is beginning to go green.

"What's the money for?"

"I'm saving it up to run away to my Dad."

"You ever run away before?"

Her eyes darken. "Yeah."

"Your mom caught you?"

"Yeah."

"Hey, Connie, give this Newbie a name," says Bobby.

Connie sniffs, rubs what looks to be a new, angry scratches up beside her ear. "I can't think of names right now."

"Call him Pointy."

"That's a stupid name."

"It's perfect."

"Shut up, Bobby," I say. Then I try to change the subject. "Connie, your mom's angry a lot, isn't she?"

Connie nods.

"She hurts you."

"Yeah. 'Cause she hates me."

"You want her to stop hating you. You want to make her happy."

"Nothin' makes Mama happy."

"I got an idea," I say.

"Pointy's got an idea," chides Bobby.

"Everybody likes cuddles," I say. Yeah, I'm grasping here, but just give me a minute, okay?

"Mama doesn't like cuddles."

"Sure she does," I say. "She just doesn't know it." Man, does that sound like bullshit. I keep going.

"She doesn't cuddle me," says Connie. "She hates me."

"Maybe she just needs some cuddle practice."

"What's that?"

Bobby and Princess Polly snort derisively.

"When does your mom go to bed?"

Connie shrugs, sniffs, tugs at her hair.

"When, Connie?"

"Whenever. I don't know."

"Does she take naps?"

"Uh-huh."

"Will she take a nap today?"

"Probably."

I bet Bobby and Princess Polly will think the idea is crazy, but I don't give a flying fuck what they think. If Connie agrees, they'll have to go along with it. Since we can't walk, where we go is up to humans.

I say, "Listen close, Connie. When Mama is down for her nap, take Bobby, Princess Polly, and me and put them in her bed with her. Cuddle us up close to her, right up against her so when she wakes up, she will feel the love."

Bobby bursts out laughing. "Feel the *love*? You been listening in to talk shows, too, Pointy?"

I don't remember where I heard that phrase but I'm using it. Like I said, I'm grasping. "Yes, she'll feel the love, Connie. That will help her get used to cuddling. Then maybe she'll know how to cuddle you."

Connie's brows furrow. "I don't know. What if putting you in her bed wakes her up?"

"She snore when she's sleeping?"

"Yeah."

"That means she's in deep. She's sleeping hard. It won't wake her."

"I dunno."

"Connie, you picked me out of a weedy patch because you liked me, right? You said so."

"Yeah."

"So trust me."

She purses her lips, looks at her feet.

Then she looks up again and says, "Okay, Pointy."

\#

Mama snores like a freight train tearing down the countryside. She's lying in her bed, flat out on her back like a corpse, drool leaking from the corner of her mouth and her eyeballs flicking back and forth behind her lids. Every few seconds, the snoring causes her head to shudder. In one hand is a cigarette, snubbed out, thank goodness. One shoe is on her foot, the other is upside down on the floor.

Connie holds all three of us – Bobby and me each under one arm, Princess Polly in Connie's hand.

"Tuck us up close," I whisper.

Connie moves silently across the floor, but I can feel the fear in her body. *Don't you dare wake up, bitch*, I think. *Stay there in stupor-land.*

Connie leans over the bed, gently places Bobby against the right side of Mama's neck. Then Princess Polly is placed on the left side of Mama's neck. I'm balanced right on top of her throat, so she can see me when she wakes up.

Connie looks at us, uncertain, but then backs away. As she turns to leave, she scoops up a couple dollar bills on Mama's bureau.

Bobby, Princess Polly, and I lie there, alone with Mama. The doll and dummy know what to do; I explained it to them.

"Hey, Bitch," I say.

Mama stirred, snores more loudly.

"Bitch!"

Mama's eyes pop open. She snorts sluggishly and stares, bloodshot eyeball to painted concrete eyeball. It's pretty clear she has no idea what's going on. Maybe she thinks she's having a nightmare. Just as well. "What the fuck? Don't look at me, you ugly piece of shit! Get off me!"

"Now, boys," I say. And cuddled there with Mama, right up close as we can be, we open wide.

Because, you see, not only can our painted mouths speak. They can also bite.

And chew.

And swallow.

Sister, Shhh

Charity did not look back. She did not slow down. Her thin white sneakers, meant for sandy pathways and wooden floors, were savaged on the rock-strewn, hard-packed earth. Her yellow dress tangled her legs and threatened to throw her onto her face.

The heat of the desert was cooling quickly, the sun reduced to an orange smear atop the mountains to the west. The sky was starless and the color of water in a deep well. Charity did her best to keep pace with her sister-wife, who was several yards ahead, but Fawn was older by a year and taller by nearly a foot.

Though she could not hear anything but her own footfalls and raspy, desperate breaths, she was sure the Prophet had roused a posse and they were thundering along behind in the darkness, truck tires biting the ground, dogs and correction rods at the ready.

Heavenly Father, help me! God, please do not curse me!

"Fawn!"

Fawn did not look back. She did not answer.

The Prophet and his men would catch them and take them to task, dragging them by their hair to show others what happened to backsliders, claiming any punishments they received at the hands of the elders were mild compared to their punishments in Hell were they to escape to live among the heathen, apostate Outsiders.

Charity's foot caught a stone and she fell, wailing, and came up with her mouth and hands embedded with grit. She scrambled up a small cactus-covered slope and skidded down the other side. The small Bible she'd pocketed before running thumped her hip, reminding her it was there, reminding her of the vows she was breaking, the chance she was taking, and the hope she might be protected, anyway.

Up ahead, Fawn's pink dress flapped like the wing of a terrified bird.

It was forbidden for girls to leave Gloryville. Females were to remain at home in the protection of God, the Fellowship, and most importantly, the Prophet. They were not to travel, nor to even speculate as to what lay beyond the borders of their holy, isolated town. They were to be submissive daughters and brides and mothers. They were to do as they were told, to surrender their bodies and souls to the men in their lives – their shepherds – who had spiritual and bodily charge over them.

"Fawn!"

Fawn called back, "Come *on!*"

An engine revved far behind in the blackness. They were coming. Charity glanced over her shoulder and saw nothing but the outlines of boulders and brambles and the quarter moon, hovering like a cat's eye in the near-black sky.

The engine sound faded, disappeared. *Maybe it was thunder*, Charity thought. *A storm coming in over the desert.*

Baring her teeth, she pushed on. Her heart hammered, her lungs drew in and out like bellows against a fire.

Then Fawn slowed. She bent over, clutching her knees, wheezing, spitting blood. Charity reached her and grabbed her arm.

"Are you all right?"

Fawn nodded.

"No, really!"

"I bit my tongue."

"Oh!"

Fawn glanced up; her eyes were creased at the edges, terrified, flashing white in the faint moonlight. But she nodded again. "I'm all right."

"We should rest. Somewhere. We can hide."

"They'll catch us, certainly. But Flinton isn't too far, I don't think. Just a mile, maybe."

Mile? I can't run another mile!

"Can you run with me, Charity? Can you be free with me?"

Can I, God? Will You hate me for leaving Gloryville? Will You punish me forever?

Charity whispered, "Yes." Fawn took her hand and they ran, into the blackness, zigzagging across the Arizona desert, heading for Flinton. Heading for freedom.

\#

Flinton had a reputation for sin of the worst kinds. Whoring. Gambling. Murders. Loud music, televisions, and a movie theater that showed films glorifying violence and sex. People dressed in clothes that revealed shoulders, midriffs, and bare thighs. Teens running the streets without supervision. Women out of their homes unescorted, drinking with each other and with men into the wee hours of the nights. Charity had heard all these things in passing, whispered stories that skittered through the sanctified compound of Gloryville like tumbleweeds on a breeze.

The men of Gloryville went to Flinton to trade, sell, and buy. It was the closest Outsider town. It had stores and banks. And so they went. But they always stamped their boots clean of Flinton's foul dirt before they re-entered their own town.

And though Charity had dreamed of escape as she lay trembling on her cot at night, she could not reconcile her longing with the fact that the only place to run to would be Flinton.

It was Fawn who first spoke the dangerous words. She had sneaked to Charity's bedside in the pre-dawn darkness before the rest of the household was awake, knelt and whispered, "I'm going to run away, dearest. Come with me."

Charity had pulled her pillow over her head, pretending to be asleep. Fawn had poked her in the shoulder and whispered again, "Friday. After prayer meeting. We can pretend to go looking for Pips."

Charity whispered into the pillow, "Why would we look for Pips? He's a faithful dog. He would never leave Rufus."

"We can hide him, tie him up so he looks to be missing. That will give us the time we need before anyone wonders where we are."

Charity was silent though she trembled so hard the cot shook beneath her.

"All right? Charity? Please? I don't want to go alone. We'll be safer together. And I don't want to leave you behind. You're the only person who loves me."

Charity felt herself nod. Fawn slipped away, back to her room, a whisper of slippers on bare floor. And Charity slept none at all until dawn, trying to breathe, staring at the wall, thinking of the dangers in Flinton, seeing images of Satan and the Prophet glaring at her, one with eyes of blazing orange, the other with eyes of ice-cold blue, wrangling over her soul.

But she wanted to leave as much as she wanted to live. And life in Gloryville had become unbearable.

Over the days that followed, Charity fought hard to keep the rest of the family from noticing her nervousness. She was certain the fear of the impending escape was obvious, etched to her cheeks and mouth like the scars cut into Fawn's shoulders from the beating Rufus gave her when she resisted him on their wedding night. Yet, as the fourth and youngest wife of Elder Rufus Via, Charity was overlooked most of the time, her ranking in the expansive family just a little higher than that of Pips.

Charity had married Rufus, a smelly fifty-eight-year-old sheep farmer, brother to the Prophet though a lesser church elder himself, eleven months prior on her fourteenth birthday. She had looked forward to the marriage and the assurance of a place in the highest realm of Heaven for obeying the expectations of her sex. She thought she knew what would be expected of her, having grown up in a family with three sister-wives and nineteen children. But her own father, a carpenter who worked hard and said little, was quite different from Rufus Via, who didn't work very hard and said quite a bit. Rufus stomped and yelled, then would disappear for several days, expecting not only the housework to be done but all the farm work, as well. If it wasn't done, or done to his liking, there was hell to pay.

The first two sister-wives, Prudence and Faith, were humble women, busy with their babies, and with little time to help Charity adjust. They assigned the youngest sister-wife the most tedious chores, as was to be expected. Laundry. Scrubbing the floors. Mucking lamb pens. Gathering eggs. Changing the diapers of their growing brood – twelve and counting, as all of the other sister-wives, including Fawn now, were expecting. Fawn, however, had taken Charity under her wing. The two girls had known each other before the marriages, had lived in adjacent homes. They'd played together when there was time to play. They'd sat near each other during the long church services that all Gloryville residents were required to attend in the windowless chapel in the center of town. Occasionally they dared pass notes back and forth, snickering silently over which boys were cute or which woman had a hole in her stockings or a bug in her hair.

So when Charity wed Rufus, Fawn was quick to give her advice on how best to submit to Rufus when he wanted her and how best to stay out of his way when he didn't.

"He wants to make you scream when he takes you," she said. "If you are silent, he thinks you aren't paying attention. If you lie still, he thinks you are in contempt of him. It's best to writhe and scream and call out to God. He may spank you with a belt, or make you do things with your mouth. Oh, Charity, just say yes to it all. Then he will be done his business more quickly and will leave you alone."

And so Charity screamed. She writhed. She prayed she would never have his child. She prayed he would die then she prayed she would die. Then she prayed God would forgive her for her prayers. She didn't really want to die. She wanted to be gone, gone far from the man and his brutal hands and body.

She peeled carrots and potatoes. She washed. She minded the others' babies. She bent over in the shed when Rufus found her there. She bore his beatings when he came to her and found she was in the midst of her unclean days. She endured his curses when she did not conceive.

And she cried on her cot in the pantry behind the kitchen. How could she stand this for another sixty years? If this was God's plan, then God was as cold and cruel as Rufus. Maybe Satan would be kinder. He certainly couldn't be much worse.

According to the whispered rumors, Satan lived in Flinton. The road to Flinton was likely the road to Hell.

And it was also the road to freedom.

\#

They reached the outskirts of Flinton and stumbled along the shoulder of the road, at a walk now, panting, sweating. Charity's hair had long since fallen free of its pins and lay like a tangled brown shawl about her shoulders. Each time a vehicle whizzed past, they shuddered and prayed it was not the Prophet. Each set of receding taillights looked like glowing devil's eyes, daring them to follow. Along the roadside were flat-roofed houses, tangled chain link fences behind which dogs snarled and howled. They passed an abandoned building with rusted gas pumps and trailers set like litter carelessly tossed, their porch lights winking. Inside, there was loud and rowdy laughter. Charity could not help but weep. Her feet were hot with blood, her face hot with dread. There was nothing left in her body but the agony of the escape, nothing left in her heart but the fear of what lay ahead.

"Sister, shhh," said Fawn. She leaned close and nuzzled Charity's cheek. "It will be all right. We just get into town, find a telephone, and call the authorities. We tell them we are runaways from Gloryville and that we need help."

"How do you know they'll help us? How do you know they won't just send us back to Rufus?"

"I've heard tell that laws of the Outsiders forbid men to marry girls our age. They believe it's criminal for men to beat their wives."

"Whose laws? Not God's laws, surely! God's laws are above the laws of man!"

"No, no! God doesn't want us beaten…"

"But if we disobey we should be beaten!"

"You're tired, Charity. Shhh, now. You want to be away as I want to. Trust me. We'll be all right. I have some coins in my pocket that I took from Rufus' dresser. We just need to find a phone, we just need to –"

And in that moment, there was a rumbling on the road, a roaring from behind, a dark growl bearing down on them, and Charity turned just in time to see a truck without its headlights on aiming at them, swelling in the darkness like an enraged monster. She felt the heat of the machine before it struck her, knocking her up from the shoulder and out into the sand. And then darkness covered darkness and there was silence.

#

"Careless, Rufus," said a man's voice. The sound cut through Charity's brain and she flinched. "Knew you took chances but never thought you'd be so careless."

Even with her face pressed into a mattress, she knew the men who were with her. Her husband. The Prophet. She could feel the sticky crust of the sheet, could smell stale sex in the fabric. In a room next door, there was muffled music, talking, laughter.

Fawn, where are you?!

"Damn women," said Rufus. He huffed and hawked, and it sounded like he spit on the floor. "What gets in to them, you know? What makes them think they can run?"

There was a moment of silence. The Prophet was likely pondering the question. Then he said, "Satan grabs a few of them and off they go. Think something's better out here."

"Out here? In Flinton? Ha!"

"Seems so."

"Bitches!"

"I won't have those words, Rufus. You're an elder and..."

"I am who I am and have always been that. Don't get high and mighty with me, Walter. I know you and I've heard your babblings ever since I was born."

"The past is past, brother. I've put up with your shenanigans for much too long. You coming to Flinton once a month for your floozies and your drink! Staying away for days, leaving your wives and children while you do God knows what with unholy women! I should have corrected you earlier, should have not allowed you to take four wives, should have..."

"Should have what, Walter? Used the law of placing against me? Or hauled me to the front of the body during worship to dress me down? Or would you have my blood atonement? Oh, I have shenanigans, all right. I come to Flinton for my fun, but I keep it away from Gloryville. I never sully our holy town. I never sully your holy name."

"Rufus! Enough."

"Enough? For who? For me? For you? Let me tell you, Prophet, should you share what I do on my own time with the flock, I will tell them of your own sins. I will tell them of the boys you have sent away from Gloryville when they reached the age. You claimed they were listening to rock music, or were caught smoking but they were innocent. We both know that. Yet off they went, banished! And I have no problem with that. We've not enough girls as it is for all the men to marry their required three. Yet what no one knows but you, me, and God is that you had your way with all the boys before you set them adrift. Oh, you savored them, didn't you, Prophet? You blessed them with your lust, rammed them into the wall of your private prayer chamber, left them limping, bloody, and torn."

"Rufus!"

"I tell the truth, brother. Shall I share that truth with the body of believers? Shall I tell the congregation?"

There was a sharp slapping sound and a grunt. Then a tussle and thud. Charity tried to turn over but her body screamed with the futile attempt.

"Hold! I think she's awake."

"You're no prophet, Prophet! You're as full of sin as the rest of the world!"

"I said hold! Stop it! She's awake, Rufus. Take care now."

"More care than your driving? You knocked her into the air, you careless idiot!"

"Not another word from you!"

The bed sank and squealed. A beefy hand took hold of Charity's chin, and turned it around. "Open your eyes, girl!" It was Rufus. Charity tried to look but could not find the energy. Though the mattress was no longer sinking, she felt herself continuing on without it, spinning, floating downward toward a soft sound of crying. A faint sound of scratching...

"I said open your eyes! You're going to listen to me, and listen well. You got yourself in trouble, girl. You're hurt and we'd got a doctor coming to look at you. He'll... I said open your eyes. Now!" A flattened palm slammed against her cheek, though she only knew it from the sound. There was no feeling of pain. Something warm spread out around the base of her gown. She thought she had wet herself, but couldn't be sure and didn't really care because...

"Damn it, Walter, help me get her to sit up."

...because her body was melting, draining like water down into hot sand, down toward the piteous crying, the scratching...

"Listen to me!"

...and all was going soft, softer...

"Sit *up!*"

....until all was calm.

All was dark.

All was silent.

#

She opened her eyes to the dark, musty confines of a closet. A slice of light pooled through the crack beneath the door. Scents of pine shavings, cigarette butts, and body odor stung her nose. She worked her shoulders, her neck, stretching against a stiffness that didn't want to be loosened.

"Uh," she grunted, and then snapped her jaws shut. If Rufus and the Prophet knew she was awake again, they would...

What? What will they do?

She tipped her head, listening through the door.

Are they still here? Did they tell the doctor not to come? Did they leave me to suffer alone?

There was no sound beyond the closet door.

Slowly she looked around. Against the back wall was a folded ironing board with the words, "Property of West End Motel, Flinton, Arizona" stenciled into the grimy fabric. A handful of wire hangers dangled on the rod above. Dead flies lay on the floor beside the dried husk of a scorpion. Little spatters of sand sparkled dimly in the carpeting.

She waited.

She closed her eyes.

Somewhere nearby she heard soft crying and a sound of scratching. She tried to speak, to ask who it was, but her voice was nothing more than cool breath on hot air.

She waited.

She heard the motel room unlock and open. Someone came in, pulling something with wheels that rattled.

Who is it? Rufus? The Prophet? What do they have planned for me? Or is it Fawn, here to help me?

A vacuum cleaner turned on and ran back and forth for a few minutes, the sound of water running in the bathroom, then the door opening, closing again.

Where are Rufus and the Prophet? How long have I been here?

She tried to open the door but her hands were too weak to work. Up on her knees, she leaned her weight against the door and shook the knob, but it did not turn.

"Help me!" she cried, but no one heard her, and no one came to help.

And so she closed her eyes and waited.

#

She came around when she heard the motel room door opening again. Two sets of footsteps, one heavy and certain, one light and shuffling.

Rufus? Are you back? Who is with you? It doesn't sound like the Prophet. Why are you leaving me here? Please let me out!

Voices. One man, one woman.

The man sounded young. He said, "Lay here, Julie. And don't you worry a bit. I'll be right back."

The bedsprings squealed. She groaned then said, "Don't fucking leave me, Bob."

"I got to. You wait here. I'll get help and everything will be okay."

"I don't feel okay!"

"Just cut it out. Don't panic. Jeez."

"I hurt! Damn you for doing this to me!"

"You did this to you, too, don't forget!"

"I hurt so bad, Bob!"

"Yeah, and the sooner I get out of here the sooner I'll be back. Here's my cell. In case…"

"In case what? I want to order a pizza? *Owwww!*"

"Damn it, Julie! I'm leaving!"

"Fine! Get the hell out of here."

"Get some sleep."

She groaned and cried out, "Fuck that! I hate you!"

The motel room door opened, shut. Charity angled her head, listening. She could hear the woman on the bed panting, sucking air through her teeth.

"Hello?" Charity called, but the woman did not hear her. The panting grew louder, more anxious. Then, weeping, moaning, cursing. Then the panting grew softer, slower.

Then silence.

Charity tried the door but was still unable to open it.

So she waited.

#

Charity heard the man come back, opening the door, shutting it. He coughed, called Julie's name, and then said, "Ah, shit. This can't be happening to me!" He left, slamming the door. It rattled on its hinges.

Charity waited. Then she said, "Hello?"

There was a long pause, then a tremulous "hello" in return.

Charity's heart leapt.

"Julie?"

"Yes. Who are you?"

"Charity. I'm in the closet. I can't open the door from in here. Can you help me?"

Julie was silent, then said, "I don't know. Let me try."

A whisper-soft movement across the rug outside the closet.

Then, "I can't seem to grasp the handle. It's like my hands don't work. What's wrong with me?"

"I think you're hurt, bad. I heard you and that man. Bob. You were angry, and you were in a lot of pain."

"I was?" There was a pause. "Yes, I was. Bob left me, didn't he? The bastard!"

"Are you still hurt?"

"Ah...no, I don't think so."

"What was the matter?"

"He'd made me have an abortion. He gets me pregnant then takes me to some fly-by-night asshole friend of his who claims to be a nurse and can do it, no cost. No cost? Too good to be true, I tell Bob. He says the guy owes him for something or other. So I figure, I don't want a kid, anyway, and the guy's got a medical degree. Or nursing degree. Whatever."

"Oh."

"But then I start cramping and bleeding like crazy. He brings me here to this shit-bag motel 'cause he doesn't want to take me home to my place, or to my Mom's or, Lord forbid to his Mom's, 'cause you know fuckin' Moms, how they can get."

"I suppose."

"I tell him, you took me to some butcher to save a hundred bucks? He says it'll be okay. He says he'll go get some real help. Why didn't he call 911? I'll tell you why, 'cause he wanted to skip town and leave me alone to..."

There was a long, dry silence.

"To what?" asked Charity.

"Like he wanted to skip town and leave me to die or something."

"I'm so sorry, Julie."

"What are you doing in that closet, anyway?"

"I'm not sure."

"What's your last name?"

"Via."

"I don't know no Vias in Flinton."

"I'm not from Flinton."

"Out-of-towner, huh? In for a one-night stand? Get dumped by your man, too?"

Dumped by my man. I guess that's what happened. Knocked down by his truck and left here until he decides to come back.

Charity hesitated, then, "I'm from Gloryville."

Julie laughed abruptly. "You're kiddin' me, right? That creepy place where the women wear those prairie dresses and puff their hair up high? Where the men marry a shit load of girls and the women ain't got no rights?"

"Well. Yes."

"You running from there? Running away to here?"

"I was..." *Fawn! Wait! What happened to Fawn?* "I was running from there, yes. They were after us, Rufus and the Prophet! We were so afraid!" Her words picked up speed as she remembered the truck on the dark road, the impact of the metal on her legs, landing in the sand. "Julie, you have to get me out of here. If they come back they'll take me home. I can't go home! Oh, my God, I think they killed Fawn!"

"What? Who's Fawn?"

"Get me out, please!"

"I can't! I can't seem to get hold of the doorknob with my fingers."

"Try again!

"I can't!"

"They could be back any minute!"

"I said I can't! I can't! I *can't!*"

"Shhh!" Charity held up her hand to silence Julie, as if the other girl could see her.

"Shh, what?"

"Listen. Do you hear that? Scratching? And somebody crying? Really soft, though, but don't you hear it?"

"Where?"

"I'm not sure. It's not in here. Maybe out where you are?"

"I don't think so."

"Just listen."

"I *am* listening! Damn, but I'm sick of people telling me what to do!"

"Sorry."

Then Julie said, "Yeah, I do hear it. Maybe it's in the other room, you think? Or the TV?"

"I've heard it before. It's the same sound over and over."

"Oh. Might be someone watching porn. Some of that S and M shit."

"What's that? S and M?"

"Never mind. You're from Gloryville, so how would you even know? Wait. Your name's Charity?"

"Yes."

"That's funny."

"Why?"

"Did you know that other Charity? The one that ran away from Gloryville, I dunno, six years ago?"

Charity frowned and put her hand to her mouth. "Who was that? I don't remember. There are a couple Charities in Gloryville."

"Girl was about fourteen-fifteen. It was in the news. Found her...shit, it was in this same motel. Crammed in a closet! She was dead, all banged up. Said it looked like she'd been hit by a car or something."

"No..."

"Never found out who did it, I don't think. Cops went out to that Gloryville, talked to some folks. Seems she ran off. Musta gotten hooked up with some bad sorts who ran her down then hid her body."

"No."

"One of the cops said that little Charity looked like she was real pretty once, in that little yellow dress and all that brown hair and a little squashed Bible in her pocket. He even cried a little on the TV. Now for a cop to cry, who's gonna forget that?"

No.

"I think the people in Gloryville said another girl ran off with her, but they never did find that one."

No!

"Do you remember either of them?"

I'm her!

"Do you?"

Oh my God, I am her!

She'd heard about ghosts. Some of her brothers talked about them privately, when they were choring outdoors. She'd overheard them, talking and giggling nervously. Ghosts were leftovers from dead people. They were spirits, free from their bodies but stuck on earth for some reason. They came out at night and shook windows and rattled doors. They could pass through solid walls and scare you to death if you looked at them. They had magic numbers they used to their advantage. Thirteen. Seven. Three. Each ghost had a purpose, but Charity did not get to hear more about that because her mother had called her back to the house.

"Hey, Charity?" said Julie. "You okay? You got all quiet on me."

Slowly, Charity stood, held her hands in front of her, and placed them on the closet door. *Am I a ghost, then? Is that what happened? Did I die here? Has it been six years?*

Her palms flattened against the splintery wood. She felt the wood grow cold at her touch, and then she pushed against it. Leaned into it. And it gave way as it if were nothing more than a barrier of fog. She tumbled forward though the door and out into the room.

Julie leapt to her feet, her eyes huge. "Oh shit oh shit!" Her blonde hair was grimy and limp, her jeans were soaked in blood down to her knees.

Charity straightened and stared at her hands. They looked the same to her. She flexed them. They felt the same but for the chill.

Julie backed toward the bed. "Get away from me," she snarled.

"I won't hurt you," said Charity. "I never hurt anyone in my life."

"I mean it! Get away!"

Charity took a step forward, wanting to console Julie, for she saw in the young woman the fear and terror that she knew had been on her own face when Rufus came at her with his correction rod or belt. And in that moment glanced over at the dresser and saw herself in the mirror.

She screamed.

Gone was the recognizable, sunburned face, the small shoulders, the slim body, and the yellow dress. Her dress was torn away at the waist, revealing ravaged undergarments. The ragged remnants of cloth were covered in black streaks and blackened blood. Her body was mangled, one arm bent with a bone protruding, her legs flayed along the shins and thighs. Her face was purpled and her jaw could be seen through a hole in her cheek.

Charity fell to her knees, clutched the remaining clots of hair on her head, and sobbed. And somewhere nearby came the sound of someone else crying softly, accompanying by a persistent scratching, clawing.

#

"We're both dead, then," said Julie. She sat on the bed, her hands folded in her lap, her brows knit, her lip trembling.

"Yes. I died at the hands of Rufus and the Prophet. You died at the hands of the nurse and boyfriend."

"So we're ghosts."

"Yes."

"I don't know how to be a ghost. What do we do now?"

Charity sat on the chair at the desk. She could not feel the seat beneath her, and it seemed odd that she did not pour right through like she had the closet door, but there was much about being a ghost that made little sense. She ran her fingers along the buttons of the phone but could not push them. She and Julie had tried several times to leave the room, only to find they were unable to step out through the door. "I don't know. Have you read about ghosts?"

Julie shrugged. "Some. Not much. We have unfinished business. I guess since we both got murdered, in our own ways."

"It seems so."

"How long have I been dead, I wonder? I would call the front desk and ask the date but we can't dial, can we?"

"I can't. Maybe you can. I've heard tell ghosts can move things sometimes."

Julie crawled off the bed and went to the desk. She lifted the receiver and gave Charity a look of surprise. She pushed the O on the dial pad. A moment later, a faint voice said, "Yes?"

Julie said, "What is today?"

"Hello? Is someone there?"

"Yes, I want to know the date."

"Hello? Hello? Who is there in room 6? No one's been in that room for weeks!"

"Please, I just want to know today's date."

"I'm coming down there, whoever you are! Intruders! Pranksters!" There was a click. Julie put the receiver down. "She couldn't hear me. She's coming to the room. Are we supposed to spook her?"

"Do you think we should?"

"I don't know. She's probably an okay lady, just worried is all."

"Then let's leave her alone."

Julie and Charity went into the closet. The woman from the front desk entered the room just moments later, and they could hear her grunting as she knelt to look under the bed, peeked in the bathroom, looked behind the drapes. Then she opened the closet door. They held still as she stared right through them. Then she muttered, "It must have been crossed wires. Must be last night's storm." She went out. Julie went back to the bed. Charity went back to sit at the desk.

"She couldn't see us," said Charity.

"No," said Julie.

Charity let out a deep breath.

"Are we stuck here? Forever?" asked Julie. "Do we have to haunt the place where we died?"

"Maybe. I don't know. I wish I did. My brothers knew a bit about ghosts. I should have paid closer attention. Oh, I hope Fawn has gone on to Heaven! I don't want her wandering in the desert, all alone!"

"Shhh, listen," said Julie.

There was the soft crying again, beneath them. The sound of scratching, clawing.

"What do you think that is?" Julie asked.

Charity shook her head. "It's what I've been hearing off and on. I thought it might be a dog beneath the motel, scampered there out of the sun, maybe."

"No, it's a human sound."

"You think?"

"Yes."

They both listened. Whimpering, scraping. Under the floor.

Charity knelt on the rug. She put her face to the floor. "Who are you?"

More crying, louder now. More scratching.

"Are you hurt? Do you need help?"

A soft, tiny voice, "Help."

"How can I help you?"

"Help."

Instinctively, Charity put her hand to the floor, through the floor into the crawl space beneath it, and felt about. Her fingers brushed against some fine, soft hair, and she gasped.

"What is it?" asked Julie.

"I don't know." Her fingers traced the hair, down to a soft jaw line, a small chest, and bony shoulder. She felt about and grasped an arm.

"What are you doing?"

"Wait."

She pulled. Slowly, carefully, drawing her hand back up out of the floor, ready to let go of the arm should it refuse to move through with her. But it didn't. The body came through, huffing, shuddering.

It was a small boy, no more than five. He had raven-black hair and brown eyes. He was dressed only in a pair of short pants. His feet were bare. There was blood at the corners of his mouth, and his chest appeared sunken, and dirt and small bits of gravel was embedded in places along his skin. He stared at Charity and Julie and looked as if he were going to cry.

"Hi, there," said Charity. "What's your name?"

He sniffed and rubbed his nose. It was then Charity saw the nubs of his fingers. He had been digging, clawing, and had worn them clear to the bone.

"Honey," said Charity. "I know we look scary but we won't hurt you. All right? We want to help you. What is your name? Can you tell us your name?"

The boy looked at Julie, then back at Charity, not seeming terrified by their appearances. He rubbed his nose with the back of his hand and said, "Nantan."

"Nantan. Is that an Apache name?"

He nodded.

"How did you get down there under the motel?"

The boy shrugged.

"Do you have any idea how long you've been down there, Nantan?"

The boy's face drew up and he began to weep again. His words were broken, desperate. "He threw me in the hole. Covered me up. Said I was nothing but trouble!"

"What man?"

"The man that build this place."

God...and how old is this motel? Thirty years, maybe? Maybe even older?

Charity tried to hug him but there was little of substance to hold. Nonetheless, she remained there on her knees, her arms encircling the boy, trying her best to replicate what had been easy in life.

Then Julie said, "Would he sleep, do you think? Could we put him to bed? Perhaps he would at least rest?"

"We can try."

Charity sat back on her heels and held out her hand to Nantan. He looked at it for a moment, as if uncertain, and then took it. Julie gently grasped the boy's other hand.

And they all felt it. A strange and sudden surge between the three of them, a blue, undulating energy that shook their dead hearts and set them pounding.

Julie almost let go but Charity said, "No, don't! Don't let go!"

"Why?"

"Just don't, please. Let's get up together."

"Why?"

"Please?"

"I guess," said Julie.

The three of them stood then, a young woman, a girl, and a little boy. Charity's brothers had said there were magic numbers ghosts used to their advantage. One was three. And here they were, three ghosts, holding hands. There was something special there.

There was power.

She led Julie and Nantan to the door.

"What are you doing?" asked Julie.

"I'm trying something." Charity closed her eyes, thought about Fawn, dead, her body God only knew where now. Perhaps her spirit lingered on the outskirts of Flinton, not knowing what happened or what to do about it all.

"Come with me," said Charity. "And don't let go of each other, okay?"

"Okay," said Julie.

Nantan nodded.

Charity pushed through the door. The others moved with her, sliding silently out onto the uneven concrete walk. The trio drifted across the night-dead parking lot, among the silent cars, as a single bat, unaware, fluttered about in search of insects.

"Wow," said Julie.

Yes! thought Charity. Together, they could go where they needed to go. Together, they would take care of the business each needed to take care of. They had all the time in the world to figure it out and get it done.

You will be avenged, sister. I may see you again. I may not. But you will be avenged. You will be freed!

Flinton wasn't so much Hell as hellish. Not so much owned by the devil as bedeviled by humans and their cruelties. Charity led the others down the road, heading westward through the shadows, casting none of their own. She imagined herself shaking the town's foul soil from her feet.

And as the sliver moon rose over the desert and dogs barked behind chain link fences, she smiled her first smile in years, savoring the expressions she would see on the faces of Rufus and the Prophet when she took them to task back in Gloryville.

Yes.

Oh, yes!

Breathe Me

The thing that had been my brother holds my face close. Red eyes blaze.

"Breathe me," it snarls.

"No!"

Its coal-hot mouth on mine, it exhales, hard.

Toxic breath spreads inside me.

I stagger, collapse.

I rise, smile.

A tottering old man outside in the alley looks delicious to us.

18P37-C, After Andrea Was Arrested

I was the last of my kind to be free, and oh, how the researchers salivated and clapped their pudgy, scientifically-purposeful hands when they stole me away from my home and imprisoned me in their silvery-clean lab. As they prodded me, probed me, and forced from me samples of hair, skin, blood, and semen, I could see the other faces of my kind, pressed to the bars of their cages, watching, their brows furrowed and their eyes dulled with depression.

I cannot live this way, I thought. Then I thought again, harder, *I cannot and will not live this way. Are you with me?*

But of course none of them could read my mind. They had not been taught to pick up such signals as Andrea and I had. And so, even though I was among my kind for the first time in my life, I was alone in my misery.

It was a snowy day when the City Protectors, in their cheerful blue suits and jaunty red caps, slammed their way into Andrea's home on a tip from someone, a neighbor maybe? A family member? It matters little now; the deed is done. The snow was impressive and beautiful as seen through our living room window, but not beautiful as judged by most humans, for, unlike rain, snow is something they cannot yet control, and this snow was inconvenient and angry, hurled from above as if from a spiteful deity. In the Protectors came in their bright blue coats and pants, tracking melting snow on the floor, already enraged at having to be out in the weather, their weapons at the ready in case Andrea resisted.

One Protector grabbed Andrea by the neck, spun her about, and slammed her face into the wall. "How dare you defy the law!" she growled as her fellow officer jabbed a shackle-shot into her shoulder. "We'll see how the courts will deal with you!"

And so it was that Andrea was drugged and dragged from our little house at the edge of the city and taken away in the human-cage vehicle as I was drugged and dragged from our house and taken away in the animal-cage vehicle.

I have not seen her again.

I will never see her again.

I am now imprisoned at RCHIA – the Research Center for Human Intelligence Advancement, its acronym pronounced "rich-EE-ah" if you care to say it aloud, though if I could speak I would find it most foul on my tongue. The room is cold, almost unbearably bright, and smells of metal tools, sterile gauze, human bodies scrubbed with antiseptics, and simian despair. There are thirteen of us caged here. One is pregnant with a future experimental subject. Our cages line the walls, and steel tables sit in the center. At any one given time, day or night, one of us is strapped down and our skulls are opened up by the "Bright Eye" surgical machine overhead. My first few days I watched what was going on.

I don't watch anymore.

I have a new name, given me by the technicians. I am no longer James, but am 18P37-C. It is tattooed on the palm of my hand and in a chip under my skin.

Here is how it all came to be, this state of affairs. Thirty-six years ago, all that remained of my kind, a scant twenty-seven of us, were rounded up in central Africa, crated, and brought back to RCHIA. The American government had paid the officials of those once-forested, drought-ravaged nations quite well, and so the leaders were more than happy to trade us for water, food, drugs, and weapons.

Since then, chimpanzees like me have been bred in captivity and used in brain research and for selective brain and spinal cell transplants into humans who have suffered major head trauma, brain diseases, or cord injuries. Even though current medical technologies make most of these transplants archaic, there are always a few wealthy people who fear such implants ("It will pervert our thinking! My dear cousin will never be the same!") and therefore demand living tissue – our tissue – that has been stolen from us, reconstituted in micro dishes, and made a suitable match for humans.

Through these sad years, humans have maintained a particular sense of morality when it comes to their own kind. People should be healed, fixed, restored at all costs. The technicians look at us with eyes too shiny with their own superiority of position and imagined superiority of purpose.

At RCHIA, my kind are trained from birth to complete various tasks, to understand and show an understanding of complex concepts, and to communicate using sign language. Young babes who reveal no promise early on are discarded; the rest are given various mind-enhancing medications and education (both aversion therapies and positive reinforcements such as trips to the compound's outdoor, tree-dotted campus) with the goal of increasing their mental powers so they will be useful down the line to donate their brain matter. A fine crop of brilliant chimpanzees to be used at the pleasure of the scientists and frightened trillionaires. In apprehension that some might learn to speak audibly, all of the chimpanzees have had their vocal cords removed as a precaution.

It is a very quiet lab, this one.

Brilliant, my co-inmates are. But brilliance succumbs to melancholy and repeated procedures and so after years of this the chimpanzees are worn out and hopeless. The "Bright Eye" takes a few more samples from them and then, like the hapless, average babies before them, they are disposed of. There is always a new crop in the making.

There has been no major outcry from the wider human population, not even from those who claim to care about species other than their own. To pacify the masses, zoological parks across the country have created quite realistic chimpanzee bio-trons that amble and gambol about the parks' large grassy enclosures to the thrill of visitors. Angela told me about these places; she has visited them. "Chimpanzees in Their Natural Habitat," the signs cheerfully proclaim. People laugh and point and hold their own children up to see the tiny, infant chimpanzees clutched to their mothers' breasts and the curmudgeonly old patriarchs pouting in the shadows or hanging from trees. Knowing that the true natural habitats of my kind are long gone – clear-cut, poisoned with toxins, and claimed by powerful warlords as their own personal kingdoms – it is accepted by the majority of humans that living in parks is better than having no chimpanzees at all. People are happy that these lovely creatures, so smart and charming, have been saved from extinction and are now protected for generations to come.

Of course, this leaves those who work in the lab free to do as they will do for the betterment of a small, wealthy portion of humankind. Their tasks are unfettered, unrestricted, and inspected by higher-ups who have similar sympathies to those who run the lab.

Andrea worked at RCHIA when she was younger. A trainee, trusted, put to work with two other technicians in the vaporizing studio. Animals that died or were euthanized were sent to them for final erasure from this world. Menial work that paid a pittance, but jobs are scarce. Andrea, all of nineteen, did her work dutifully until the studio received two newly dead chimpanzees, and one, Andrea discovered, was carrying a fetus that had reached a viable stage of development. Andrea was surprised that the scientists had not noted the fetus, or had decided to ignore it, even though it would have been quite easy to keep the mother in a state of suspension long to bring the fetus to term.

But when Andrea inquired about the fetus she was 1. told that the mother had died of an accidental overdose of a particular chemical which would have quite seriously and negatively affected the brain development of the fetus and 2. told that she needed to keep her questions to herself; her job was to get rid of dead bodies, period, not second-guess anything or anyone.

With a scalpel she rescued the tiny being – me – and spirited me to her home at the edge of the city. I remember very little of my first months, except that I was warm, tenderly cared for, and safe. Andrea explained to me later that finding me was a startling moment in her life, a time of epiphany. She could no longer work in the service of death. She left her position at RCHIA, and began painting wild, bright, and glorious landscapes from her imagination, lush and vivid as might have existed in the 20th or 21st centuries. Many people found her art to be trivial, delusionally fanciful. But there were enough who found her fantasy paintings to be appealing or at least entertaining. Those were the patrons who helped Andrea make a living, even if that living was minimal.

During the first months of my life, Andrea taught me sign language (I was in no way brain damaged from my mother's overdose) and games of strategies. I quickly came to understand her spoken language as well as her signed language, and we became the best of friends.

She named me James.

Over time Andrea developed a passion for ancient religions and mystic spiritual traditions. She immersed herself, and read to me many nights the teachings that most impressed her, passages from revered texts that moved her soul and mine. She embraced the concepts of compassion that were the core of these religions. She chanted and sang; she blessed other beings she encountered from one day to another. She practiced the art of controlling one's breathing and heartbeat with the power of the mind, and became quite skilled at this for it brought her into stillness and quiet. With great patience taught me the same. Some evenings, after tea, we would sit silently on the floor, and become nothing for a minute or two. When we returned, we were refreshed and at peace. We even trained ourselves to catch portions of each other's thoughts when focused enough on one another.

I was safe with Andrea. I observed the greater world through her window and through the readings we shared. At times I felt a faint genetic longing for the wild, but was satisfied with the cloistered life I had been given.

Andrea's art shifted from landscapes to sky-scapes and what she imagined could exist out and beyond what we knew for certain through so many years of far-reaching exploration. I tried my hand at painting, but not every soul can express itself outwardly through art. My artwork was quite ridiculous, but I enjoyed the laughing as did Andrea.

And then we were discovered, Andrea arrested, and I was caged at the RCHIA lab.

Voiceless despair, hopelessness, and dread.

There is no sound quite so horrible.

The first one I was able to reach was 17P24-C, whose cage is next to mine. She is twelve years old and newly impregnated. She had dry, drooping lids and lackluster fur that had come out in patches where she has repeatedly and furiously groomed herself. Using the sign language we both understood, I told her it was time to resist. I saw in her eyes a hint of soured bemusement, and she turned away. It took another several weeks to get her to understand what I meant, and for her to finally admit that I was right.

Patiently, and in time, she convinced the other chimpanzees, though several were very resistant until the full impact of our plan dawned on them. Then, we became of one mind, one heart, one purpose.

With hand signals and spellings, I taught them, as Andrea had taught me. The technicians didn't follow our communications, for I was careful and subtle as I signed through my bars.

And we practiced.

Even as we were taken out and cut and stitched and returned to our cages, we practiced.

Even as some of us lost bits more of our mental faculties, the portion of the brains that remained were able to focus on the plan.

We practiced slowing our breathing, slowing our hearts until they nearly stopped, becoming nothing, and then returning, with a new sense of what peace might mean.

Becoming nothing and then returning.

Nothing, and returning.

The technicians kept on with their work. Feeding us, tinkering with the "Bright Eye," experimenting and cutting, complaining as they always did about the tediousness of their jobs, fussing about their wives and husbands and children, gaining nothing from their lives that could even smack of peace.

This morning, 17P24-C began to sense the fetus within her, moving, stretching, and told me immediately. The baby was not yet viable, and we knew time was of the essence. I alerted the others. They were ready. All thirteen of us exchanged knowing, relieved nods through the bars of our cages around the room.

We have reached the moment to act.

Practice is over.

We are ready.

We wait until the technicians are standing by the counter near the door, drinking coffee and rambling on about some sort of sport on which they had all placed bets. Arguing over which team was fastest, strongest, most clever. Laughing, scratching, stomping about in their little white shoes.

I look at those of my kind, their eyes prepared for surrender and happy for it. They look at me. I give the sign, a simple hand gesture, a finger pointing ceiling-ward. Sky-ward.

I think of Andrea.

We focus on our breathing. It slows. We focus on our heartbeats. They slow. We will become nothing.

And this time, we will not come back.

Peace.

Peace.

The Darkton Circus Mystery

Peter Darkton's Traveling Circus of Wonders was a sad little spectacle, hardly a circus and not even enough to qualify as a mid-list side-show, hauled about by a 22-year-old Chevy Suburban with large rust spots and a 1975 30-foot travel trailer with bad shocks and a long gouge down its side where Peter had backed it too close to a row of pines in a Kentucky campground. Peter traveled throughout the year, deep South in winter, North in summer, and as far west as Illinois whenever he could afford the gas and the weather held. He was fifty-eight now, well-worn himself with spots and gouges from an occasional fight with locals who came to his exhibit drunk or who just wanted to test their manliness again a stranger who was, more often than not, shorter and less muscular than themselves.

But the traveling circus was a living. A living handed down from Peter's father, who'd inherited it from his own, and so on back into the fogs of the long, forgotten past. And just as they had when his ancestors parked their horse-drawn wagons in weedy-choked pastures or beside muddy river banks, when Peter parked his Suburban and trailer in a campground or in the trees along a graveled country roadside, they came. They came with crumpled dollars and twitching noses, drawn in by the garish paintings on the side of the trailer showing costumed monkeys playing cards, a vanishing pig, chickens dancing in a spotlight, and most curious of all, the big, fire-red letters promoting "The Darkton Circus Mystery! See It to Believe It! Feed It! Prove Your Courage! Then Speak Of It To No One on Pain of Certain Death!"

On this particular September day, Peter had the circus rattling up the western slope of a Virginia mountain, seeking a lonely place where people hungered for an entertainment beyond the everyday, hoping the vehicle's slipping transmission would hold. In his lap was a bag of corn chips, in the drink holder a beer he'd wrapped in tin foil. In the passenger's seat was his daughter, Kelly, aged seventeen, who'd joined him when he'd swung through her hometown of Dillyville in northeastern Tennessee and told him she wanted to ride with him for a month or so.

"This is exciting!" she said, her feet crossed and wriggling, her eyes trained out the windshield. "Mama said I'd never get away from home, said I might as well get used to working at the Hilltop Motel like she does. But look at me! Heading out to see the country with you."

Peter grunted then glanced at the rearview to make sure the trailer would make it around a particularly sharp mountain curve.

"Where will we stop?" Kelly asked. "Where do you plan on setting up today?"

"I know places when I see them. It just happens."

"Oh, that's fun. I like that idea!" She nodded happily, and then picked up some of the fast food trash on the floor at her feet, balled it up, and stuck it into a half-empty bag. She was a tidy one, Peter's daughter. "I'm glad you agreed to let me come along. We can get to know each other like real family. Great, huh? Thanks. Dad!"

"Don't call me Dad."

She frowned, looking a little hurt. "What, then?"

"Just Peter."

"Hmm. Well, all right. Peter."

"You gotta shush now, you hear me? I have to pay attention to the road."

"Okay. Will do."

She was so damned agreeable.

As it was, Peter hated the idea of Kelly tagging along. And he hadn't planned on stopping in Dillyville but he knew that Carol, Kelly's mother, still had the hots for him after all this time, and he was in need of a little something warm and wet besides his own spit-slicked hand. Carol had obliged – and she did have a most comfortable bed – then was pissed, as he expected, when he refused to take her out to breakfast the next morning.

But Kelly, who hadn't seen Peter since she was ten, had followed him out of the apartment to the Suburban, asking sweetly to come along, offering to cook and telling him she had nearly $700 she could get out of the bank on their way out of town. So, of course, he couldn't exactly turn her down. And now, not quite a day's travel with her, he'd already spent her down to $587. Gas. Chips. A case of beer. Motor oil. A new-for-him coat and pair of boots from a Salvation Army store in Big Stone Gap. Kelly didn't seem to mind.

In fact, she didn't seem to mind any of Peter's requirements and restrictions.

"When I got the radio on, no talking," he'd ordered when she first climbed into the vehicle with her sleeping bag and pillow. "I want to listen to a game or a preacher or music or weather, you be quiet, you hear me?"

Kelly had nodded.

"And I sleep in the middle seat where it got more room. There's no room in the back-back 'cause of the cookin' gear."

"No motel?"

"Of course not. I ain't made of money,"

"Okay."

"So you get the front seat. You're short and small but you'll fit. Just adjust the steering wheel up as far as it'll go. And don't ever get out in the middle of the night 'cause it'll disturb me. I need my sleep."

"Okay."

He'd started the engine and pulled away from the apartment complex as Carol, on the walkway in her terry robe and dog-chewed slippers, had shaken her middle finger and shouted "Asshole!"

A few miles out of town, he'd said, "There's one part of the circus you are to stay away from, never open up, never even try to get a peek."

Kelly had glanced at him. "What's that?"

Peter continued. "I know you're scared of snakes, Kelly. Always were. I don't know much about you now, but I do know that."

"Yeah. I don't like snakes one little bit."

"The last display in the trailer, the Darkton Circus Mystery, is a snake. A big snake, largest one you'd ever see. Under no circumstances are you to mess with that display. You are never to try to get in there to have a look at it. I don't need you having nightmares or begging me to take you home before I'm ready to go back through Tennessee. You understand?"

She'd nodded solemnly. "Okay."

And so they continued on into the mountainous wilds of Virginia, seeking a venue both isolated and peculiar, talking rarely, Peter trying his best not to fart in the Suburban but unable to alter his habits, and Kelly, when talking was allowed, telling him about her life since he'd missed most of it.

She was a plain girl, thoughtful, and sensitive. She was used to being poor, she told him, used to being ignored, used to working as a companion for an old woman with dementia in the evenings and a maid at the motel during the day, and used to giving most of her money to her Mama to help pay the bills. She knew Peter was disappointed that Kelly had not been a boy, because he'd wanted a son to give the circus to when Peter was too old to travel. She didn't think he'd pass it on to her because she was a girl and that wasn't how the family did things, but said she hoped he'd reconsider.

"I could do good with a circus," she said as they rumbled along a narrow valley between two mountains awash with October red. "You could teach me how it works, how I can be part of it, you think?"

"Huh."

"Maybe?"

"Shush now."

They rode in silence another few miles. Then Kelly said, "Mama doesn't like you much. But I think she just doesn't understand why you are like you are. I kept telling her she must have loved you once, and she that she still should even if you aren't together. And you're my father, so of course I love you."

This hit him like a pocketknife to the neck. "Don't say that again."

"Why not?"

"It's just wrong, is all."

So she didn't say that again.

Peter found the spot he'd watched for, a flat, thistle- and vine-covered acre off the road three miles from the nearest town, nestled between a creek and a sheer rise covered in kudzu and granite outcroppings. Peter could stay here until someone came and kicked him off. He figured he'd get at least two good nights' worth of ticket sales.

While Kelly set up the Coleman stove and got a stew cooking, Peter prepared for the evening show.

One side of the travel trailer was covered with the colorful headlines and artwork. This is the side that Peter always parked facing the road, facing traffic. The other side, which Peter always situated facing away from where customers would park their cars and trucks, was divided into sections with 3' x 4' doors that unlatched and folded down, revealing the displays inside each compartment. The first section had two little capuchin monkeys that, on command, dealt a deck of cards on the floor then picked them up and put them down as if in a game. The monkeys were getting up there in age, bought from a pet supplier in Maryland, and Peter just hoped they could make it through another season. The second section held three chickens that, when Peter turned on his CD player, would scratch on a brightly colored spot on the floor while a little silver, faceted ball spun overhead, mimicking a disco. In the third section, mirrors and lights made it seem as if a pig (a taxidermied pig that had died a number of years ago) disappeared except for his floating snout. All this was ordinary carnival fare.

But the last section of the trailer was different. It did not have a pull-down panel to reveal what was inside the compartment but rather an actual door, a door with a lock opened by one of the keys Peter kept on a string tied around his neck. The windowless room inside was big enough to hold four to six customers, and two cages, one small, one large, one covered in an old towel, the other covered by a blue velvet curtain. In the little cage were stray pets Peter collected along country roads or stole out of farmhouse yards when it was clear the owners were not home. He taped their mouths shut to keep them quiet. It wasn't as if they would starve to death like that; they never lived that long.

In the big cage was the Darkton Circus Mystery, Peter's joy, his terror, and his inheritance. While chickens, monkeys, and pigs died and were replaced or stuffed, this display lived on. It brought Peter respect. It caused others to fear him. The money was minimal but that was because to keep the show to himself he had to maintain a low profile. If he went to a big city with this treasure, it would be broadcast, highlighted, and then swept out from under him like everything else of value was when people with big money caught wind of something they wanted.

Peter hauled the canvas tent out from the rear of the Suburban, unrolled it, and hoisted it up into place against the back side of the trailer where the displays were located. It was hard work but he was used to doing it alone. In fact, he enjoyed the sweat and burn the work created. It reminded him that he wasn't dead yet, in spite of the years that had been piling up. And so when Kelly offered her help, he declined and told her to just stick with the cooking and if she got bored, she could listen to the radio.

When the tent was propped and pegged and roped nearly all around, Kelly peeked around the edge of the trailer to tell him dinner was ready.

She stared at the tent as Peter wiped his hands on his coat.

"Why a tent?"

"People come to see the shows," Peter said. "With the tent, only those who pay can see the displays as I reveal them one at a time."

Kelly nodded, then shivered. "I suppose that snake in the last display scares them mighty bad, doesn't it?"

Peter nodded.

"It must be a mighty big snake. Is it ten feet long? Fifteen?"

"No talking about it, Kelly."

"Twenty feet long?"

"Leave it be."

"The sign says nobody can talk about it once they see it or they'll die. Is that true?"

Peter glared at her. "I said enough. We'll eat now."

"Okay, sorry." As they moved on to dinner, he noted Kelly glancing over her shoulder, fear flickering across her features. He would have to make sure things stayed that way. No way in hell could he let her know the truth.

#

Kelly agreed to serve as the ticket taker; she was happy to do it. As quiet as she most often was, she knew how to deflect the advances of drunkards and slicks. Her mother had had her share of such boyfriends, all puffed up and oiled down, and Kelly had long ago devised a way to make them shudder and turn away. She would loll her head and slobber a little, and the men would jump back a good three feet and move on.

So there she sat at a little card table outside the tent with a roll of tickets and a metal cash box, smiling at the customers who seemed harmless and letting her head wobble and the spittle drool a bit for those who had ill-intent brewing at the corners of their eyes. And so they all left her alone, giving her their dollars, taking their tickets, and moving out of the night-shadows and into the tent-shadows.

Peter stood by the tent, nodding and smiling at the customers, then at last entered and pulled the flap down, sealing them all within. Kelly sat outside at her table, batting away the gnats and listening as Peter, in a surprisingly strong, commanding voice, explained each of the first three exhibits to the groans and complaints of the customers. Several stormed out, pausing at Kelly's table to demand their money back. But Kelly gave them the cock-headed drool and they turned and went on. The rest stayed, however, charmed by Peter's promise of what was in the last section of the trailer, the big Mystery, even though they'd have to fork over another ten dollars each.

At last, Kelly could hear the trailer door scraping open, the customers stepping into the trailer and causing it to rock on its shocks. The door creaked shut. After a long pause and some more thumping around, she heard the customers wail in fear. Their words were muffled but clearly terrified. Peter said something low, ominous. In another few minutes the customers were pressing out through the tent flap, clutching their hats, glancing around furtively, fearfully. Even those with ruddy complexions looked paler, their eyes pinched and their brows drawn. They stalked away, not speaking to one another, climbed into the various vehicles, and took off into the night.

Then, over the sound of late season crickets and owls in the trees by the river, Kelly thought she heard a low growl within the trailer, a heavy, guttural sound that made the hairs on her arms stand up. And she heard Peter say, "Shut up, you!"

A moment later Peter exited the tent, mopping his brow, pushing a loose strand of hair back from his forehead. He stared at Kelly as if he'd forgotten she was there. Then his lip hitched. "You got the money?"

She held up the cash box.

He took it, shook it, and then held it like it was a baby. She wondered for the briefest moment if he ever held her as a baby. Probably not.

"That's good," he said. "Now you go on back to the Suburban, go to sleep. I've got business, got to lock up." He pulled a cluster of keys out from his shirt, the keys that hung around his neck. "And you got any peein' need to be done, you do it before you get to sleep. As I said, no getting up in the middle of the night."

Kelly nodded, and then before she could stop herself, said, "Those men must be scared of snakes, too. I can't imagine how awful that snake must be."

Peter pointed a finger at Kelly. "Yeah, it's damn awful."

"And loud. I heard it make noise. A growling sound. Like a dog or bear. Gave me goose bumps."

"No more about the snake! Don't never speak of it again, you hear me? Or I'll leave you on the side of the road."

"I'm sorry. I won't."

"All right, then."

"I don't want you angry at me."

"Then don't make me angry."

"Okay."

Peter blew air threw his teeth and glanced at the sky, where clouds were beginning to break apart, revealing a spattering of stars against the dark. Kelly thought for a moment she saw him sigh and soften just a fraction, but then he straightened, huffed, and strode into the tent with the cash box.

He didn't trust her. It made her sad. But there was time. Surely, there was time to get him to care for her, to need her, out here on the road. And that was all she wanted. Someone to need her.

#

When he was certain she was settled in the Suburban, curled up on the front seat in her sleeping bag, he took care of the final business of the evening. As was sometimes the case, the five customers who'd paid extra to see the Darkton Circus Mystery didn't have enough money to buy food to feed the creature. And so now it was up to Peter to take care of the feeding. He hated it; he preferred keeping the curtain over the cage and not having to look the thing in the eye any more than necessary, but business was business and to make his living with the circus, he had to keep the creature alive.

Peter stepped inside the room at the end of the trailer and pulled the door shut, closing off the night air and the bugs that seemed determined to follow him around. He flicked on the light switch and faced the large, curtain-covered cage. The thing inside the cage began to thump about, and growl.

"Shut up," said Peter.

"Like I'm going to do anything you tell me to do," said the creature. The curtain billowed slightly at his voice. "Now give me some nourishment, you ridiculous old redneck. How long do you think I should have to wait? You're getting slower and slower in your old age. Your father was much more conscientious than you are. Your grandfather, though, another worthless bit of flesh on two feet. Just like you."

Peter's neck flushed as it always did. More than thirty years of hauling this thing around and the insults still stuck in his craw. Still, he had to feed the thing. He couldn't let it die.

He took the towel off the top of the small wire cage, pulled up the lid, and removed two puppies. They struggled in his grasp, kicking at the air, their taped mouths twitching. They stared at him with confusion and fear in their tiny brown eyes. That confusion would be over soon.

"Here you go, you old freak." Peter flung back the curtain on the cage and crammed the puppies through the bars. The creature, unable to stop himself, snatched them up from the floor and, one at a time, buried his long, needle-like teeth into their necks and drained their blood. Then he tossed the carcasses back out through the bars. His huge, yellow eyes narrowed. "More."

"No more," said Peter. "You know that. I give you more, you get stronger. You get stronger, you can pull some of that shape-shifting shit and get out of here. I'll give you just enough to keep you breathing, living...well, living's not quite the word now, is it?"

The creature growled and lashed one hand through the bars just as Peter skipped back.

"You know," said the creature. "I can smell that young girl on you. Who is she, a little tart you're fucking?"

Peter blinked then curled his lip. "My daughter." The moment he said it he knew it was a mistake. "Don't ever speak of her again."

"Ah, a daughter. I had a daughter once. Lovely thing. Delicious blood. Drank her dry then threw her body out for the vultures."

"No, I mean it. You speak of her again and I'll down your rations even more. Or…" He tipped his head in the direction of the plastic lunchbox nailed to the wall on which the words, "Safety Kit," had been written in white paint, "…I'll snuff you out as you sleep during the day. I can do that anytime I want, you know. Easy. No sweat."

"But you won't, Peter. You need me. Just like your daddy and your worthless granddaddy needed me. Without me, your show is nothing. Without me, you are nothing."

"Shut your fucking yam hole, freak." Peter jerked the curtain back down over the big cage. Then he tossed the towel over the small cage as the kidnapped pets bumped around inside and whined.

"Damn, what I put up with."

Certain the door and latches were locked and the cash box was stowed in the back of the Suburban, Peter situated himself in the middle seat and pulled his ratty wool blanket up to his chin. He never had a pillow but used a balled up sweatshirt he no longer wore because mice had gotten to it somewhere along the line. It was nearly midnight, and he needed his sleep. What a hell of a day, this traveling with company. He hoped he could survive the interruption, at least until Kelly's money ran low. Then he would let her off – put her out – in some town where she could call her Mama to come get her. He'd give her a few of her dollars back, of course. She was an okay kid, for a kid.

He flopped over, wriggled around to get comfy.

Happily, at least, Kelly didn't snore.

#

It was still dark, but she had to pee. Bad. She sat up in the front seat, her eyes sticky from sleep and her back hurting from being pressed against seatbelt latches that refused to remain tucked beneath the cushions.

Crossing her legs hard, she wondered if she could force the need away. She counted, one, two, three, four, five, six, seven. But it did no good. She had to go.

Quietly, slowly, she opened the Suburban door. Luckily, the overhead light had burned out, but there was a faint, grinding squeal of metal against metal. She grimaced and looked over the seat to find Peter sound asleep with a sweatshirt under his head. His chest rose and fell against the blanket. His mouth hung open as if inviting a spider. She pushed the door again, slowly, and then eased out onto the ground. Leaving the door partway open so it wouldn't bang shut, she tiptoed across the field to the trees where she relieved herself, found a couple dried leaves to finish off, and then sneaked back to the vehicle. The dead grasses and weeds crunched beneath her feet. Overhead, bats stitched patterns against the pre-dawn sky.

It was then she heard the moaning. The agonized groaning. From the rear of the travel trailer.

Pathetic.

Agonized.

She stopped and stared at the trailer, at the garish signs on the side, black and white and shades of gray now, their colors washed away in the night.

The sound came again, and then a thumping inside the trailer.

"What is that?" she whispered. The sound of her voice was louder on the air than she'd expected.

There was a moment of silence and then again moaning.

Weeping.

"That's no snake."

She took another step toward the Suburban, but the sounds from the trailer were heartbreaking. She bit her lip then hurried to the trailer, around the side, and into the tent where she stopped to listen again.

The crying was louder now but no less pitiful. It came from behind the closed door, the final display.

The gigantic, terrible snake.

But she knew snakes. They didn't cry or moan.

So what was it?

Kelly patted her fist against her teeth. Clearly there was someone in the trailer, someone who, for some reason, had been locked inside without Peter's knowledge. Was it a child? Had any children come to the show? She didn't remember any. The voice was difficult to identify. Maybe it was a teen, or even a man, who was horrified to have been left behind without being noticed, locked inside the trailer with the dreadful snake.

Peter would be so pissed if he realized he'd been so careless. She didn't want him angry. She wanted to make things better for him, not worse. And she couldn't leave that poor soul trapped in the display. Just the thought of it made her stomach clench and her heart pick up a heavy, painful rhythm.

The keys were around Peter's neck. She would make quick business of it, not even have to go inside the trailer but just open the door for a moment to let the man out.

Peter was lying face toward the back of the middle seat, snorting in his sleep, one hand twitching, but luckily the string on which the keys hung was visible at his neck. And the fingernail clippers she kept in her purse did the trick. He never moved, never felt a thing.

Back inside the tent, standing at the door now, Kelly trembled. The keys clicked against each other like tiny teeth. This had to be quick. This had to be quiet. Once she freed the trapped person she would tie a knot in the string of the key and drop it onto the Suburban floor where Peter would find it in the morning. She would tell him how he tossed and turned all night, possibly scooting out from under the string in the process.

That was possible, wasn't it?

It was the best she could think of.

The moan was so loud this time it drove her back several feet from the door. Maybe the person was already bitten by the snake? Maybe he was lying there, dying. She hoped not. She knew how to put on a Band-Aid but that was about it. She didn't know how to stop someone from dying.

Go on now, she thought. *Do it. Do it for the man. But most of all, do it for Peter. Do it for your Dad. He needs your help.*

God, I hate snakes!

"One, two, three, four, five, six, seven, eight…"

Key in the lock, lock clicking, door pulling open slowly, as quietly as possible.

The room was very dark, and it had a disgusting smell. Dead things. Piss. Shit. She covered her nose with one hand and squinted, trying to get her eyes adjusted.

"Hello?" she whispered. "Who's in here? Can I help you?

The sound of her voice stirred up other sounds, small sounds of whining and scratching.

No, that's no snake.

Shut up and just do this, Kelly!

She took two steps into the trailer, keeping her free hand on the doorsill.

"Hello?"

Things began to take focus. A small bin or cage against one wall, covered in a lumpy towel. That's where the whining was coming from. To the right was a huge cage covered in a curtain. The uneven hem of the curtain revealed the bars at the bottom.

And a pair of scuffed black shoes pressed up against the bars.

"Oh, shit," Kelly whispered.

"Help me," said a raspy, desperate voice from within the large cage. "Please, help me."

"I…" began Kelly. Where the hell was the snake? Was it in the cage with the man who was speaking?

I can't look. I can't do this…

"Please, help me!"

Kelly licked her dry lips but they remained dry. "Is…is the snake in there with you?"

"There is no snake," said the voice. "I'm here alone. Locked up. Trapped. Your father did this to me. Please, please let me out!"

Kelly drew back. "What? No. My father's a good man. He wouldn't lock someone up."

"He did. You don't know your father very well."

"He said there was a snake in here."

"There is no snake. That was a ruse so you would stay away and not come help me."

"No, he wouldn't do that to me. He wouldn't lie."

"You are a loving girl, I can tell from your voice. I've been captive a long time. I fear I will die if I have to stay locked up. Please, please set me free. I won't press charges against your father. I just need to get out."

Kelly bit her lip, looked at the door then back at the curtained cage.

"I…"

"Please! Help me!"

The voice cut her with its angst, and she could no longer resist. Stealing herself and taking a breath of the dank, acidic air, she pulled back the curtain.

He stood there, tall, broad shouldered, hair jet black, face skeletally angular and as pale as the moon. But it was his yellowed eyes that drew a gasp from her, his dreadful gaze that locked with hers and caused her heart to stop beating for two, three, four counts before it was able to pick up again. He smiled at her. The smile was horrific.

"You want to know who I am," he asked, and though she did she was unable to nod. "I am your father's great mystery, his great assumed money-maker, which is a farce, a ridiculous, centuries' old joke, for neither he nor his family have made squat displaying me, they have only delayed the punishment that my captivity will bring upon their heads."

Kelly could not speak, she could not blink, she could not look away from the man with the yellow eyes. He tipped his head and considered her, then raised a brow. "You have come to change all that."

She could not reply, she could not scream. She could only stare at him, locked face to face, and feel her sense of self fade away.

"Open the cage," said the man. "You have the keys."

She felt the keys in her hands, though could not look at them.

"Now!"

One by one, she fumbled with the padlock on the cage door.

"Stupid, slovenly slut," he hissed. "You're like your old man. A simpleton."

Then Kelly pushed the correct key into the lock, and with a snap, it came open. The man chuckled darkly and pushed his way out of the cage.

"Now then," he said.

She looked at him, stared into the yellow eyes, wanting what was there but not wanting what was there, waiting to see what would happen to her next, because she knew she had no choice in the matter.

He took her by the shoulders and said, "Ah, now." His breath was rancid, like old butter and bad meat. He opened his mouth and she saw the shining, needle-like fangs there. She did not pull away. "Time to regain my strength. It's been a while since I've had a good, long drink. Hold still, dear."

She did.

He leaned forward, pushed her hair roughly from her neck, buried his fangs into the flesh, and he drank.

He drank.

She slipped to her knees and still he drank.

She felt her knuckles strike the floor, and then her forehead, and still he drank.

#

It wasn't quite daybreak when Peter woke up, and she wasn't in the Suburban. And she'd left the damn car door open and the bugs were inside, all over the place. He had gnats in his nose, and he sneezed them out onto his sleeve.

"Where the hell is she?"

Probably out to pee, couldn't wait any longer. He thought young people had stronger bladders than that.

He struggled out of the blanket, climbed from the Suburban, and relieved himself against the front tire.

Then he noticed that the string of keys was no longer around his neck.

"Shit, oh shit!"

He fumbled around inside the vehicle, dug in the cushions, felt along the floor among the balls and bits of trash. But the keys were not there.

"Damn it to Hell! Kelly!" he shouted. "Where are you?"

She didn't answer.

"Fuck!" She couldn't have taken his keys. She would not have done that. She said she respected him. She was a good girl, a kind girl. She wanted to please him.

"Kelly!"

He rolled out of the Suburban and stormed around the trailer to the tent. No way would she have disobeyed his rule. No way would she have tried to see what he told her not to see. She was a tender-hearted soul. She wanted to do good. And she was afraid of the snake he'd lied about.

He entered the tent. He saw the last exhibit's door standing wide open.

"Oh, fuck!"

He didn't want to look.

And of course, he had no choice.

She was there, inside, lying on the floor, her hair tacky with dried blood, her eyes open and staring at a dust clot just inches from her nose. On the side of her neck were two brutal, raised puncture wounds.

The big cage was empty.

"Kelly!"

He dropped beside her, picked her up, shook her. "Kelly!"

There was a faint stirring inside her body. She was still alive.

"Kelly?"

The last town they'd driven through was too small for a hospital, but surely there was a doctor. A doctor who could do a blood transfusion? Someone who could bring her back around.

"Kelly?"

Kelly shivered, groaned.

"Kelly!"

And then her eyes turned toward him. They were a ghastly yellow, putrid like piss-filled pools. She grinned a dead woman's grin, and he saw the needle-like teeth.

"Oh, my God!"

He dropped her, leapt to his feet, and clawed open the plastic safety kit, keeping his gaze on Kelly, who was now staggering to her feet and snarling, "I smell...your blood. I....I am hungry."

Peter removed the sharpened stake and wooden mallet from the box. He held them up. "You did this to yourself, damn you! You ruined my show! You freed the Darkton's Great Mystery! How am I going to tell your mother that I had to drive a stake through your heart?"

Kelly shuffled toward him, groggily grinning her terrible grin, her lips hitching. Peter poised the stake before him, the mallet at the ready.

But in that instant he realized he had to explain nothing to Kelly's mother. He realized that he'd lost nothing, really, but his temper and a little time.

He tossed the stake and mallet aside and shoved his still-wakening daughter into the cage. She fell hard, growling, slashing with her fingers, snapping her fanged jaws. The lock was slapped into place and locked. Peter stepped back. Breathing hard, and considered his handiwork.

"This'll do," he said.

Kelly's lips formed a sluggish, "No...."

"Yep, sorry, dear. You brought this on yourself. You wanted to be part of the circus, so welcome to it. I'll give you enough to keep you alive but not enough that you are a danger to me."

He pulled the curtain down and left the trailer.

Outside the tent, sunlight was creeping through the trees, washing the field, and awakening the songbirds.

Kelly would be falling to sleep right about now.

Peter lit the Coleman stove, opened a can of Spam, cracked a few eggs, and cooked an omelet. It was messy, but oh, quite tasty.

The Tree

There is a tree in the park. It is an ordinary tree. Or rather it looks like an ordinary tree. An ordinary oak tree. It's tall, about 50 feet. It stands at the far side of the park, past the benches, the swing sets, and the sliding boards. Past the picnic tables and the ball field. It's light green in the spring. Dark green in the summer. Red in the fall. Naked in the winter.

People don't often go as far as the oak tree. Parents keep their kids close to the benches and the swing sets and the sliding boards. Families eat at the picnic tables and play on the ball field. And so the oak tree just stands and grows all alone except for the squirrels that eat the acorns and nest in the branches.

Little Joey Jones never did what he was supposed to do. He was always getting into trouble. Always doing this or that, or that or this, driving his mother crazy and making some of her hair fall out.

His Mama took him to the park one day. She sat on a bench. She took Joey by the shoulders and she said, "Joey. I'm tired of you misbehaving! Now I want you to stay on those swings where I can watch you. Don't you go running off, now! I mean it!"

And of course little Joey thought making his mother chase after him would be great fun. He swung on the swings for a minute. Then he ran over to the sliding board.

"Joey!" shouted Mama from the bench. You see, she was a very tired woman and once she sat down she did not like to get up again. "Joey, you come back right now!"

Joey didn't come back. He climbed up the slide and slid down. Then he climbed up the slide and slid down.

Next he ran over to the picnic tables. There was a couple having fried chicken and potato chips for lunch. Joey grabbed up some chips and stuffed them into his mouth as the couple just stared.

"Joey!" shouted Mama as loud as she could from the bench. You recall, she was a very tired woman and once she sat down she did not like to get up again. "Joey, leave those people alone! And come back right now!"

Joey didn't come back. He snatched up a chicken leg, made it do a little dance on the picnic table, and then took a big bite.

Next he ran over to the ball field. Some high school students were practicing batting and catching a ball. Joey caught the ball and ran around the bases with it while the teenagers chased him.

"Joey!" screeched Mama from the bench. Remember, she was a very tired woman and once she sat down she did not like to get up again. "Joey! Give that ball to those kids! And come back right now! I'm not kidding! I mean it, mister!"

Joey didn't come back. He threw the ball as far as he could throw and then ran to the far side of the park where the oak tree stood. He stopped and looked up at the tree.

From way back at the other end of the park, he could hear his mother yelling from the bench. You may have heard that she was a very tired woman and once she sat down she did not like to get up again. "Joey!" Mama yelled. "Get back here right now! Now, Joey, or you'll be sorry!"

Joey did not go back. He stood looking at the oak tree. "I'm gonna climb me that stupid old tree," he said to himself. "I'm gonna climb that stupid old tree and make it mine! Mama can't tell me what to do!"

A squirrel came up to Joey. She blinked and said, "You better do what your Mama says, Joey. She knows better than you."

Joey frowned. "Does not, you stupid squirrel," he said.

"Does, too," said the squirrel.

"Does not," Joey said.

"Does, too," said the squirrel.

The squirrel shrugged her little shoulders and said, "Suit yourself, then." She scooped up an acorn and had a bite.

Joey went to the bottom of the tree and looked up. The tree was full of red leaves that swayed in the breeze. There were other things, too, small round things dangling from the branches. "Those are stupid-looking acorns," laughed Joey. "A stupid tree, stupid squirrels, and stupid acorns!"

Then he began to climb. Hand over hand he went, up, up, up into the old oak tree. He passed several squirrels along the way. They just looked at him and shook their heads.

At last Joey reached a branch he thought would make a good seat. He wiggled and squiggled himself down onto the branch and grinned. "This is my tree now! I'll sit here and look out over the park. Out over the ball field and the picnic tables. Out over the sliding boards and swing sets. Out to the bench where my mother is sitting and waiting for me. She can worry all she wants! She can yell and her hair can fall out and I don't care! Ha ha ha!"

Then he reached out to pick an acorn. "Stupid squirrels eat these things," he said. "I wonder what they taste like?" But then he looked at it closely. He screamed.

It wasn't an acorn. It was a tiny little head with the face of a boy about his age. The boy's mouth and eyes were opened wide in terror.

Joey flung the tiny head away. He sat shaking on the branch. Then he looked up and around him. Every single acorn was not an acorn at all. They were all tiny heads of kids, some a little older, some a little younger. They stared at him with silent, horrified eyes.

"You should have listened to your mother," came a voice behind Joey. He spun around, nearly losing his balance, to find a squirrel sitting beside him.

"Who....who are all those kids? Those faces? Those little acorn heads?" asked Joey.

"It's like this, Joey," said the squirrel. "There are always some dumb kids who just don't care about anything. They never do what they're supposed to do. They leave their Mamas behind and ignore them. Those kids scare their Mamas and make their Mamas' hair fall out. Those kids come here and climb up in our tree like they own it. We warn them but they ignore us. So now we own them."

"But...but aren't their Mamas worried when they don't come back?" whimpered Joey.

"No," said the squirrel. "When we turn you into acorns, the Mamas forget they had a kid. Then they go home and make themselves a nice jelly sandwich."

The squirrel held out her little paw. Little sparks jumped from the tip.

"Leave me alone!" screamed Joey.

The little paw touched Joey on the nose and POP! He became one of the many little heads hanging in the old oak tree, swaying silently in the breeze.

And Mama left the bench, went home, and made herself a nice jelly sandwich.

My Treat
(a poem)

Upon a knoll, beyond the town, amid trees dark and bent,
A long-forgotten house stands mute, porch broken, curtains
    rent.
The windowpanes are greased with filth and crossed with
    splintered cracks,
The floors are warped; the walls are iced with ancient,
    melted wax.

It is this place I call my home and have for countless years,
My birth was here, my life, my death, my agony, my tears.
Doomed by a curse upon me on a long-past Hallow's Eve,
Though I am dead, so yet I live; I rage, I long, I grieve.

Alone, alone, within the damp and darkness of this cell,
Unable to escape its hold, forever, this my Hell.
The cellar, attic, halls, and rooms I must remain within,
Shuffling, snarling, cursing, longing, weighed beneath my
    sin.

Yet on that night of frosty stars and winds that howl and
    sigh,
The night when shadows hold themselves and dead leaves
    start to fly,
I peer beyond the broken glass, my eyes, unblinking, wait,
To see them venture up my path and rattle at my gate.

Their costumes hide them, keep them safe, or so they do
    believe,
They come to the forgotten house, so young and so naïve.
Nervously they giggle as they step upon my porch,
Eyeing cautiously the vines, the spiders' webs, the torch.

And there, within the opened door, seated all so still,
Am I; my red eyes, staring, give the visitors a chill.
They dare each other, Who'll be first to reach out for the
    treats,
And take them from those ghastly hands, that mannequin in
    sheets?

The treats are little bits of things I've found about the place,
A button, ribbon, patch of cloth, a string, a bead, some lace.
It does not seem to matter to the children at my door,
Each year they come to test their wits, to goad, to brag, to
    roar.

I hold and do not move as each one, trembling, in his turn,
Leans forward, and, so carefully, as if fingers will burn,
Snatches up the bit of something with delicious dread,
And there! The barest brush of living flesh against the dead.

When each has had his turn, they leap and scatter down the
    path,
Rolling far and out of sight with scream and shout and
    laugh.
Then they are gone; I close the door and shamble to my bed.
I stare out at the ghost-gray clouds and gold moon
    overhead.

'Twill be another year until the Hallowed Eve comes 'round,
'Twill be another year for me to hear the blessed sound,
Of human footstep, human voice; and what I long for, much,
That fleeting, warm, sensation of a living human's touch.

Sickle Moon

I'd really done it now. Mama was gonna to be so pissed off if she found out. That was *if* she found out. But she wasn't going to. I wasn't going to let her know. Not this time. This time, I was going to fix it for good. Get in that kind of trouble again? Nope. As Mama likes to say, "Fool me once shame on you, fool me twice shame on me."

I ain't no fool.

It was August, and hot and sloppy as an old cow's lips. Everything stunk – my clothes, the house, the tool shed, the tall grass in the field where groundhogs had died from some kind of groundhog disease. The river that runs behind our house stunk, too. Dead fish was snagged along the banks in the weeds, their eyes popped like water balloons. Butterflies had committed suicide and peppered the river's surface in spatters of yellow and orange.

Lots of things was dead that summer. Like them groundhogs and butterflies. Like my newborn baby.

I had the baby yesterday, in the morning after Mama drove into town where she works at the grocery store. She didn't know I was pregnant. Nobody did, not her, not my younger sisters or my dumb-ass ex-boyfriend, Jeff. Just me. I'm no skinny girl, so it wasn't hard to hide my belly beneath a big shirt and loose shorts. I just went on with things the way they was and didn't say a word. I wasn't even showing 'til school let out in June, so it was easy to keep my mouth shut and wait for it to happen.

And it did, 'bout one o'clock yesterday morning. Water busted at three, and the pains was really bad by five-thirty. Mama got up to go to work at seven-thirty and I just stayed in the upstairs bathroom and listened to the car rumblin' down to the road. My little sisters whacked on the door, screaming they had to pee, but I just said I had the diarrhea and they'd have to use the bathroom off the kitchen or go the fuck outside behind the shed.

An hour and a half later, the baby was out. I was sweating, bloody, my gut aching and my pussy was sore like I'd been dragged over gravel. I crouched between the toilet and the tub, unable to stand. The baby was on the bath mat; a boy. It was gummy and wrinkled, with little cracks for eyes and a little pink mouth.

It looked a lot like my first baby, except that one had been a girl. The girl I'd named Lily Joan because I thought I'd get to keep it. This one I wasn't going to name 'cause it died right after it come out of me.

With my legs bowing beneath me, I finally pushed up, swiped the mess from bathroom pretty good, and then took the bloody towel and baby to my bedroom. I put the baby and towel into the backpack I used in ninth grade last year. I crawled into bed and slept into the night. Mama came home, knocked on my door and I said, "Go away, I got the flu," and so she did. I went back to sleep and slept through the next morning.

It was two o'clock in the afternoon. Mama was off to work and my sisters was watchin' Jerry Springer. I stuck my cell phone in my back shorts pocket (we ain't got no reception where I live but there is some in town and at school, too, and I hate to be without my phone no matter what) and sneaked out through the back screen door. I walked through the field toward the river and the woods beyond. I let the backpack slap through the waist-tall grass as I went.

ShuWhapShuWhapShuWhapShuWhapShuWhap.

I stepped on a black snake with my sandal and it spun away into the weeds in a blur of oily muscle. Clouds of mosquitoes hung above the grass, waiting for an idiot like me to walk through them. I tried to wave them away. Damn bugs, can't imagine what God was thinking.

Mama had freaked out last time I had a baby. That was summer a year ago. I knew I was pregnant, and I was dumb enough to tell Mama. She wanted to know the daddy's name but I wasn't going to tell her because the daddy was her boyfriend, Don. Don had come to visit her one Friday night in the fall. My two sisters was spending the night with their friend Dorrie. I was home with Mama 'cause nobody'd asked me to the eighth grade Harvest Dance.

Mama had got mad at Don for saying something stupid and sent him home with a fryin' pan to the side of his head. I was on the front porch as he stormed out the door and down the steps. He stopped on the walk and looked back at me. He asked me didn't I have a date to the school dance and I said I didn't want to go to a stupid dance, anyway. He said did I want to take a walk and we could both commiserate. I wasn't sure what commiserate meant but I didn't really want to sit on the front porch anymore so I went walking to the field with him. We talked about school and my mom, and then he said I was pretty for a fat girl and kissed me. Soon we was lying in the grass with my panties around one ankle and his clammy parts in me.

The baby was born in July, and Mama was pissed. She took it away from me and went to the kitchen. When she gave it back, it was dead. She said that was good. "We don't need no damn baby," she said.

I didn't like what Mama had done. I said, "I could'a given it away."

She snorted and said, "Nobody should have nothin' that's ours, even if we don't want it."

She told me to get rid of the baby's body. So I took it out into the woods and buried it. Not too far, just past the river to the big oak that has that old hunting blind up in it. I didn't want to go any farther, though, 'cause I knew witches lived deep in them woods somewhere.

Mama grounded me for three weeks for having a baby.

Now I'd gone and had another one. Mama would ground me forever if she found out. I wasn't going to let her.

I reached the river and rolled my shorts up to my ass. I held the backpack over my head and picked my way across, wiggling the toes of my sandals into the pebbly riverbed. A dragonfly hovered over my head for a moment before scooting away. I don't like dragonflies. One girl back in fourth grade said they was little spirits sent by God to watch to make sure we don't do bad stuff.

On the other side of the river I shook the water off my legs then took an overgrown path into the woods. This was one of the many trails hunters used in the fall during deer season. The path led through the forest about a quarter-mile and ended at a large oak tree that had an abandoned, plywood huntin' blind nailed up in it.

Even the woods smelled bad that day. Maybe a bear had dug up Lily Joan and had left bits of her laying around in the heat.

I couldn't bury my second baby this close to the first one. If somebody found pieces of the first one they might go snoopin' and find the second one, too. Two dead babies would send some busybody whining to the sheriff. The sheriff would pull some of that CSI shit and find my ass out. Our governor had sentenced kids young as sixteen to death for murder. I didn't want to get grounded and I sure didn't want no lethal injection.

I had to go deeper into the forest, follow Ivy Creek and then beyond some more to where I'd never been before. That way, no one would look, no one would find, and no sheriff would care.

But the witches, they had a cabin out there somewhere. Two witches they was, twins, at least a hundred years old, probably more. My ex-friend Margaret said she'd seen the witches' cabin once when she was out hiding from her drunk dad. She heard them cackling and crept through the underbrush to have a peek. She saw their cabin in a forest clearing. All the plants was dead around the cabin. There was a dog on a chain, and it was nothing but a bone-white skeleton with a few hunks of dry skin on it. Margaret said it was lying on the ground but she was sure she saw it move and snarl at her.

I'd have to make damn sure I didn't cross the witches' land. I'd have to keep my eyes open and my nose up so I could smell them. Witches smell like rotten milk and puke, Margaret told me.

I found Ivy Creek, and followed it as it wound back and forth. Its banks was thick with raspberry bushes and poison ivy. The backpack snagged on the brambles and my legs got scraped with thorns. But I had to follow the creek or I'd get lost for sure. I stumbled and cursed along the creek, until it took a sharp right. Then I left the creek and moved up through the trees and thorny greenbrier, hoisting the backpack from one shoulder to the other. I was almost far enough to bury the baby. Just a few more minutes and I would be shed of my mistake. Then I could go back home and make prank calls to Margaret's house to piss her off. I heard she'd been telling lies about me down at the Texaco where kids from school hang out during the summer. Fucking bitch. I never slept with Michael Pugh like she said I did. Michael Pugh was a pimple-face moron. But lots of kids believed Margaret. I would get her back, though, that was for sure.

The ground rose steadily, and I panted as I climbed. My feet slipped in my soaked sandals. Pine silt clogged the spaces between my toes. Damn dead baby, making me do this much work.

I reached the top of the rise. There was a large, grassy clearing and a fence traveling as far as I could see to the east and west. The fence was made of splintering rails and twisted barbed wire. Little bits of hair was caught on it every few feet – deer hair, fox hair, and some that even looked like people hair.

I stood by the fence, squinting in the sunlight. It took about five minutes to catch my breath from all that hikin'. Yellow jackets spun about my head. Then a wind whipped up from below, and it smelled like rotten milk and puke.

Oh, fuck it all! The witches' cabin's somewhere nearby. I might be on their land already!

I looked in all directions. There was nothing on the knoll but weeds, a few saplings, and the wire fence. The ground sloped down on all sides for about fifty yards to where the forest started again.

Where was the witches' cabin? How close was it? What did they look like? Did they still have that skeleton dog on a chain, ready to growl at intruders and bite their feet off?

Then I thought, *What would witches do if I found their cabin and threw the dead baby in their yard and ran away? They'd eat the baby and there wouldn't be no evidence left, that's what they would do. Witches liked eatin' babies better than regular people liked eatin' ice cream. Says so in the fairy tales!*

That was the perfect idea. Let them witches have the baby!

The backpack started to shake. Startled, I peeked inside and nearly shit my shorts. The baby's legs kicked and its closed eyelids wriggled.

What the hell?!

The baby trembled, making little mouth movements like it was trying to cuss me out but didn't know the words for it.

Then, it went still. Maybe it was really dead this time.

I scanned the knoll, trying to decide which way to go, when I heard a high-pitched cry to the east, down in the trees. I tipped my head and listened. It came again. It was a woman, and she was cryin'. Hard. Like she was hurt bad.

Maybe she was attacked by the witches. If I find her, she can tell me what they'd done to her! I'll get some good pictures of her wounds and Margaret'll be jealous as hell, 'cause she ain't never met somebody that survived a witch attack!

I hurried through the tall grasses as fast as I could go, dragging the backpack, following the fence line down to the trees.

ShuWhapShuWhapShuWhapShuWhapShuWhap!

I saw here before she saw me. She was a dried-up woman with long gray hair curly as Spanish moss. She was tangled in the barbed wire fence. Shadows from the sycamore branches strummed her as they waved back and forth, like she was some old string-less banjo. My breath snagged. My heart drove its fist against my ribs.

Damn! That ain't a witch victim! It's one of the witches, herself!

I crouched low behind a sapling. I pulled my phone out of my pocket; I was gonna get a picture then sneak back away real fast and quiet.

Then the baby in my pack whimpered. The witch heard it. Her head snapped about and she looked straight at me behind the sapling. The phone slipped out of my hands and down into the weeds.

Shit!

Her eyes was huge and watery as rotten goose eggs, and her open mouth black like the bottom of our old well. I could smell her breath. Rotten milk and puke. We both screamed at the same time.

Then the witch said, "Girl!"

I said, "Don't talk to me!"

The witch said, "Girl, get me out of here!"

I said, "Don't talk to me! Witch's voices is poison! Shut up!" I dropped the backpack and put my hands over my ears.

"No, no! I ain't a witch!" cried the witch. "I'm trapped! I fell into the fence and can't get out!"

I could hear that damn witch through my hands.

"Listen to me!" she cried.

I lowered my hands. I didn't say anything, but I didn't run away. My legs was shaking, but I didn't run. She was stuck, that witch. Stuck and beggin' me instead of throwin' curses at me. Ha!

"Girl…you ain't got no idea what's after me," she said. Her old tongue went out of her mouth and wet her wrinkled lips. "You got to get me out of here 'fore nightfall."

"Why I gotta do that?" I asked. "Why I got to help you out before nighttime?"

"Tonight's the sickle moon!"

"So what?" I couldn't believe I was challenging a witch, but it felt really good. "No moon never hurt me!"

The witch took a ragged breath. "You don't want to know what the sickle moon means out here in the woods. Help me! You look like a nice young lady!"

I put my hands on my hips. "I ain't nice! I'm a kick-ass female! Ask anybody, they'll tell you!"

"Ah," sighed the witch. She tucked her old head down, and it looked like she was crying again, but this time I couldn't hear her.

I picked my phone up out of the weeds, stuck it in my pocket, grabbed the backpack, and moved closer. Margaret would have thought that was a really stupid thing to do, but screw her. She's the stupid one. I moved to the tree line and had a better look at the witch. She was smaller than I thought at first, but just as ugly. Flesh hung on her face and neck like skin on a ham that's cured too long. I could see she really was tangled, cut and bleeding. Looked like part of her lip was missing. She wasn't going anywhere fast. She stunk much worse close up.

"Please...you gonna help me?" asked the witch.

I didn't answer. I inched even closer. When I was a few feet from her, she coughed, long and hard. "I was...runnin' last night," she managed, "and I couldn't see where I was goin'. Came along here and then the fence reached out and grabbed me down. It wrapped me up in its barbs. You got to cut some this wire away of me, all right? Then I can roll out and go on my way."

I spit on the ground. "You tryin' to trick me to get me close! Fence reached out and pulled you down? Ha!"

"It did," she insisted. "Sharp things are spiteful."

"You's a pretty crappy witch. You's a stupid, lyin' witch, matter of fact."

"I ain't lyin'."

"Witches got spirits that can get them out of anywhere. Where's your spirit at?"

"I'm not a witch at all," said the witch.

"Oh, yes you is!" I almost laughed. "And where you hidin' your witchy sister?'

The witch's face twisted at that. "My sister?"

"Where's she at?"

"Cabin."

"Where's your cabin at?"

"Other side...of the knoll," the witch mumbled, nodding only slightly so the wire at her throat wouldn't dig deeper. "Child, we can talk about this later?"

"No, now!" I barked. "Tell me about you and your witchy sister if you want me to untangle you!"

The witch's eyes narrowed and her face darkened. I thought any second fangs would come popping out through her pressed lips. *Here comes the curse*, I thought, and I got ready to run.

But she said, "We ain't witches. Ain't never been witches."

"My stupid used-to-be friend Margaret said she saw your cabin. Heard you chantin' some witchy-shit and saw your devil dog skeleton on a chain."

The witch shut her eyes just for a moment. It looked like she was praying. Probably to ole red-dicked Satan himself.

Then in a voice crusty as a dead leaf she said, "My name's Molly Marshall. My twin sister's Annie. We've lived in our house since we was born. My father raised pigs. He died young. Our mother died old. We've always lived in the cabin."

"Ya'll curse 'em to death?"

"What else you need to know 'fore you let me free?"

I had her by the girl-balls sure as the fence had her by the flesh. "You want out, you gotta teach me a spell first."

"Get me out!" she wailed.

I crossed my arms. "First, teach me a spell I can use. A really good one I can use on my Mama."

The witch swallowed hard. Her voice was now faint and quivery. "It'll be dark in just a few hours. The sickle moon's watchin'! It's comin' soon! You can't believe what that'll mean for you *an'* me! *Please!*"

I was starting to feel damn good. Stupid witch, too dumb to stay out of razor wire. Me, standin' over her like her queen. "Teach me a spell!" I ordered.

She took three deep breaths then her old watery eyes rolled up in their sockets. Her head fell back, her mouth flopped open, and she muttered through a glob of spit, "Sickle sharp, sickle cold, cut cut cut cut cut cut!" I thought she was teaching me a spell so I started to repeat after her, "Cut cut cut cut cut!"

Wind stirred around me suddenly, spinning hard, jerking and knotting the ends of my hair and throwing silt in my face. The sound of the wind and the creaking tree branches was that of dark laughter. A cloud passed over the sun and a chill scrabbled up my spine.

"Cut cut cut cut cut cut cut cut cut!" babbled the witch.

No, wait, she wasn't teachin' me a curse. She was cursin' me! Aimin' one right at my soul while I stood there like a rubber-legged turtle!

I spun around to get the hell out of there. But something wiry and sharp snatched 'round my ankle and jerked me backward, hard. I crashed flat on my face. My thoughts blew up flew away like ashes from a bonfire.

When I came around, the forest was dark, except for the faintest moonlight floatin' on the weeds around me.

I looked at the sky beyond the sycamore branches. It was black and salted with stars. At the edge of the sky was a silver sickle moon, curved and sharp. The stars mixed up with the ones in my brain and spun crazily. I tried to sit up and but hammer inside my skull drove me back down. I touched my face and found a wet, throbbing, pulpy thing there. "My nose is broke!"

A weak, breathy voice near me said, "We got to get out."

It was the witch. I remembered. I was in the forest on top of the goddamned mountain, lying next to a goddamned witch caught up in a goddamned wire fence. My nose was broke, and maybe even my ankle. I still hadn't got rid of the baby. And Mama was home, pissed for sure, ready to ground me 'til Kingdom come or worse. Probably send that ass Don out lookin' for me!

I glanced over at the witch. Her face wasn't three feet from mine, saggy and cut and old and nasty, staring at me buggy-eyed.

"Get me out." Her breath curdled the air between us.

"I can't stand! My ankle's screwed up!"

"You best get up...or..."

I heard it then, a heavy thumping through the ground – steady, slow. It sounded like Don stompin' around in those hillbilly clodhopper boots he usually wore. Mama had sent him to find me, to take me home to face the music. He would drag me back to Mama so he could get in good with her now he wanted her back.

I got to get up! Don ain't gonna take me nowheres!

"Oh god!" wailed the witch in the fence.

I ain't goin' home 'til I'm ready to go home! Nobody gonna make me!

My palms pressed against the uneven ground and I pushed myself up. My nose pounded. My ankle stung worse with my weight on it, but I was getting the hell out of there. I'd give that witch one good, quick kick in the head before I took off. I balanced myself, lifted my good foot, and aimed at her face.

But then I saw a shadow rising up in the trees 'bout ten yards behind the wire-trapped witch, and it froze me dead. The shadow huge and was blacker than the night around it, a massive shape darker than darkness. And I could smell it – a rotten stench so thick I was almost knocked backward.

The witch craned her head around, too. She saw the shadow and began to whimper. "Oh, no no no!"

Ever so slowly the gigantic shadow arms reached out, creaking and groaning like tree branches in a storm. They were unnaturally long, like what an alien mutant spider would have, and in the right hand was a sickle. The curved blade caught the dim moonlight and winked hideously. My heart kicked into high gear.

Shit shit shit!

I grabbed my backpack and wrapped my fingers tight around the strap. I could run fast with two good ankles, but I only had one. I needed something to slam into the monster to knock it off its feet so it couldn't get any closer.

I whirled the pack and heaved it out with all my weight behind it. But the strap caught and the pack flipped back around, hitting the ground by my feet.

There was a click and bright flash in the monster's right hand.

And then I could see.

"Hi, there, honey," said the one who had cast the shadow. It wasn't a monster at all, not an enormous spider-armed creature, but a little old woman. She had braided gray hair and wore a raggety dress with a white apron with a big front pocket. She wasn't holding a sickle in her hand, but a flashlight. By her side was a small black dog with tick-thickened ears and a lopsided grin.

"I see you found my poor, lost sister!" said the old woman.

I wasn't no fool. She might look like a nice old lady but she wasn't, no sir! My lip curled. "You's the other witch! You's Annie!"

"Witch?" she said, her eyes twinklin' in the glow of the flashlight. "Is that rumor still going 'round? How many generations now, thinkin' the two of us is witches? Makes me sad." She looked down at her sister. "Molly, why'd you run off? And look at you now, all slashed up in that wire fence!"

Molly shrunk back.

"Let me help you," said Annie.

"Don't touch me!" shrieked Molly. She drew back, deeper into the razor wire, tearing several new slashes along her face and arms.

Annie looked at me again and sighed. "Molly gets scarit real easy. Poor thing."

I looked at the woman in the fence and the woman in the apron. I saw the truth and even though it wasn't scary anymore, it was real disappointin'. "You two really ain't witches, are you? Just two old ladies, one real crazy and the other just real old."

Annie pursed her lips and shook her head as she gazed down at her sister. "That wire fence is strong stuff. Daddy put it up years ago to keep the pigs from runnin' away back when we owned this mountainside. Made sharp angles out the wire and posts, back and forth, back and forth. Cuts deep and won't let a trapped pig go. Hold it tight 'til it's time to take it home and slit its throat for supper. Sharp things got their own agendas."

"You don't make no sense," I said.

"You ever see what they can do, sharp things?"

"Whatever, you old cunt," I said. "I'm out of here."

"Hold on," said Annie. "And take a look at this." Annie stuck her hand in her apron pocket and pulled out the biggest damn curved knife I ever seen. A sickle – sharp, shiny. There was some weird carvings on the wooden handle.

What the hell?

"You like this?" Annie asked. "So nice, so sweet. It tells me what to do. It talks to me. Soft, secret words it says." She smiled a big smile and her teeth looked nearly as sharp as the sickle. Then she ran the blade of the sickle along her finger, opening up a flap of flesh that bled red and thick. *Ew, sick!* I cringed, but she just looked at it and nodded. "I can hear it now, whisperin' to me, sayin' you and Molly is next. It has needs, you know? Can I ignore it? 'Course not!"

Crazy-ass freak!

Annie's dog was no longer grinnin' at me. He was sneering. His teeth was locked tight and his lip was pulled up like a window shade. Fur on his back was raised high. He moved out from Annie, head low, as if ready to jump on me any second.

This was the worst shit I'd ever stepped in. I had to get away. "Gotta get home," I said, slippin' on my backpack.

"Can't stay and chew the fat. Sorry. You have a good day, now."

The dog circled to my left, trying to block me from leavin'. From the corner of my eye I could see a sagging place in the fence next to Molly that was low enough for me to climb over. But I didn't know where to run if I went that way. I'd be lost for good.

Goddamn!

The dog snarled, its ears flattened against its head. Annie waved the sickle at me. Molly whimpered.

Annie's gaze moved from me to the sickle. She touched the blade with her bloodied finger, like she was in love with it or something. "Oh," she groaned. "Oh oh oh oh." Her eyelids fluttered. She began to rock back and forth. The dog's attention moved from me to its master. "Oh oh oh oh oh..."

I slowly swung my leg over the low place in the fence, keeping an eye on Annie. A barb snagged my crotch but I moved on and over with a tug, clearing the wire with my other leg. My mouth was dry as dirt; my nose ached and my ankle throbbed. But those was the least of my problems.

From the ground by my feet, Molly whispered, "Get me out an' I'll get you away safe, down to the main road. I know these woods. You don't. Annie's in one o' her trances. She's no witch but she's crazy as a loon, and dangerous under the sickle moon! If we don't move now, though, she'll come out of her spell and have us both!"

Damn! Okay, fair enough.

I dropped to my knees, wrapped my fingers around the cloth strap of the backpack, and tried to pull the wire away from Molly's shoulders. It wasn't budging. She said, "Reach in my dress pocket, got me some kitchen shears." Her shirt was twisted 'round, the pocket away from her own entangled hands. I carefully slipped my hand inside and pulled out the sheers. They was small, but sharp and sturdy. I snipped the wire on her neck. It curled back, releasing the skin. I snipped again and again, taking chunks of fence away from her shoulders, her arms, her legs. On the other side of the fence, Annie groaned and said "oh oh oh" and "I hear you, my love!" over and over again. My hands were clammy and shook with the task. Three times I got gouged by the wire and the cuts set my skin afire.

Then Molly was free. I grabbed her beneath her sopping armpits and hauled her up. She didn't weigh but a mite and at that moment, I couldn't care how bad she stunk. Her feet scrabbled and then got beneath her. She said, "Follow me!"

We ran, Molly leading more quickly than I could have guessed and me following. The pack clapped my back with every jarring step. My ankle screamed but it wasn't gonna stop me. We raced through the brambled darkness, Molly calling "log!" when there was a log and "rock!" when there was a big rock so I could dodge 'em or hop 'em. Branches slapped me; soft spots in the ground threatened to suck me under, but I ran after the old woman, down and down, around and around, away from her insane sister and her pet sickle. My lungs fought me but I kept going. The skinny, curved moon popped out of its cloud cover and watched through the trees like an excited kid holding his breath.

Then there was a small log house ahead in a clearin'. A low, red light glowed through a front window. Molly ran across the barren front yard and onto the porch, waving madly for me to hurry and join her.

"Where's the main road?" I sputtered. "This ain't the main road!"

"Another mile, but we can hide here a bit! Catch our breath."

"Here?" My legs pushed me forward onto the porch but my mind was tryin' make me stop. "What's here? Is this your cabin? You think I wanna hide in your cabin?"

"I got a phone, you can call home."

"I got a phone! Ain't no reception up here, you liar!"

"We got a landline. You can call home, or the police. We can lock the door 'til they come. Annie's lost her mind and she needs to be put away. Police'll come, or your Mama'll come and save us. Hurry!"

I went into the cabin with Molly. As Molly locked the door behind us, I leaned over and wheezed. My heart was thunderin', my ankle was wailin', my nose was throbbin', and my leg bones was threatenin' to break like twigs.

After a few moments I forced myself to straighten up and look around. It didn't seem much like a witch's cabin, which was good. There was a saggin' sofa, a big wardrobe, a small table, a single window, and a fireplace where dying cinders sizzled behind a rusting screen. A lantern sat on a table beside the sofa, casting a puddle of light onto the floor. Molly crossed her arms over her dirty dress and watched me from beneath her shag of gray hair.

"Where's the phone at?" I demanded, adjusting the backpack on my shoulders.

Molly said nothing.

"I said where's the fuckin' phone? I gotta make that call before your sister gets here!"

Molly stepped close to me and started to giggle.

"Did you hear me?"

Molly put her hands to her mouth and tittered like a brain dead kindergartener.

I slapped her face. Her head rocked back and forth on her skinny neck, but she kept on laughing.

"Where's the phone at!?"

"This is so much fun!" giggled Molly.

A voice from another room said, "Ain't it, though?"

Then Annie came out into the light of the parlor with her big-pocket apron and holding her god-awful sickle. Her grin was huge and yellowed. The dog was beside her, his grin equally large, equally tainted.

"I'm out of here, bitch," I huffed. Dread and exhaustion made my voice squeak, and it sounded pathetic. There was no way I could run away. I wouldn't make ten feet before they'd be on me.

Annie reached for the lantern, turned down the light.

The room went dark.

Thin moonlight drifted like dust from the window and settled on Annie. She threw back her head and moaned "oh oh!" like she was comin' hard. Then the moonlight went to work on her, changing her, stretching her, morphing her. Her features dissolved into darkness and she grew taller, wider, rising up, becoming the impossibly huge shadow-monster with freakishly long spider arms. Fire-bright eyes winked in the faceless face, teeth as sharp as a bobcat's clicked. The sickle waved in her – in its – hand. The room was filled with the hot, foul stink. The dog moved to its master, and as it did its skin bled away, leaving a growling skeleton.

I screamed.

"Sickle sharp, sickle cold, cut cut cut cut cut cut!" wailed the Annie-monster so loud the window glass rattled.

"Cut cut cut cut cut cut cut!" cried Molly.

The Annie-monster smiled its vicious smile. "Do you hear it? Yes, I hear it! Cut cut cut cut cut!"

"Do we hear it?" echoed Molly. "Yes, we hear it. We shall do it! Cut cut cut cut!"

Molly moved to one of the wooden wardrobes. "See the spoils of many sickle moons!" she shrieked, and she yanked the wardrobe door open. Hanging inside on tarnished hooks were countless heads, strung together like bulbs of garlic, eyes closed, lips slack, flesh severed at the base of the neck. Some were shriveled like mummy heads. Others were fresher. I recognized one. It was Margaret, with her stupid '80s hairdo and teddy bear earrings, gazing out with eyes what couldn't see me no more. I guessed she'd decided to have another up close look at the witches. The other heads was hillbillies or hunters or morons what got lost on the mountain.

Bile burned a path up my throat. I managed, "You killed all them people?"

"We obey the sickle moon," said Molly and Annie-monster at the same time, with the same voice. "We do as we're told. And in return we're given life, power, to live forever. Cut cut cut cut cut cut!"

I backed toward the front door. The skeleton dog snarled. Molly and Annie moved toward me, side by side, pressed together. I stared in horror as Molly's old lady body melted and was absorbed into her sister's, creating an enormous two-legged, two-headed, four-armed beast. The giant spider arms coiled and twisted as they reached out for me; the sickle flashed back and forth.

"Hold still now, won't hurt," both mouths said. "You'll join the others so fast...so fast your head will spin!" The heads screamed laughter.

I yanked on the door lock. It didn't budge.

Goddamn it!

I stumbled out of the reach of the conjoined monster witches. I yanked my backpack from my shoulders and hurled it to the sofa. The Annie-Molly monster turned in unison toward the sofa. All four sets of sharp teeth chattered cheerfully.

"There you go!" I shouted. "Have at it!"

Fucking witches!

"Baby flesh!" they cooed, instantly distracted. "We've got no babies in our collection." They shambled to the sofa and knelt clumsily. Two of the hands unbuckled the strap that held the pack closed while the others held the sickle and stroked it tenderly.

I reached the window and drove the heels of my hands against the glass. Like the locked door, it held tight.

Open open open! I willed the window. *Let me the fuck out!*

It would not give. It was painted shut.

At the sofa, the Annie-Molly monster had opened the back and had lifted the baby free of the towel. "Mmm," they said together, their dark, shadow heads bobbin' all excited-like.

The baby squawked. Its eyes blinked and its fists batted the air. It made a noise that sounded more pissed than anything else.

Damn baby, I thought. *Just like me, hardheaded and not willing to die!*

And suddenly, I didn't feel alone. I had my kid. *My* kid, not noboby else's! We was in this together. Mama was right, nobody should have nothin' that's mine! Fuck 'em!

As the monster admired my baby in preparation for the kill, I hurried behind the wardrobe and shoved with all my strength. It fought me, but I fought back. I pressed my feet against the wall and pushed. It teetered then crashed forward, taking the strings of heads with it. The wardrobe slammed down onto the two-headed shadow monster and knocked it flat. The baby fell free and bounced on the sofa. The monster wailed and kicked beneath the wardrobe but the sickle stayed tight in one hand.

I screeched in triumph and grabbed up my baby, who stared at me and then closed his eyes as if satisfied. I said to the demon on the floor, "Gimme that damn sickle!"

The two heads said nothing, but the sickle lashed out at my legs.

Swish! Swish!

I was going to have it. They wasn't goin' to cut off no more heads. I stomped the hand with the sickle and the blade bit into the flesh of my ankle.

Shit, another fucked up ankle!

I cried out, stomped on the hand again, and the grabbed for the sickle. This time it came free. And at that moment both heads closed those fire-bright eyes and those sharp-toothed mouths.

They died as silent as moon-wind.

The skeletal dog whined and laid down beside its mistresses. Then it just up and died, too. Yeah, I know, that a dead dog can die sounds weird but no weirder than the rest of the shit I'd just gone through.

Limping on my bad ankles but holding my baby close, I went to the lantern and turned it up. In the light there wasn't nothing 'neath that old wardrobe but two old women with Spanish moss hair and saggy, ugly-ass faces.

"Well," I said, standing tall. "Ya'll brought it on yer damn selves!"

Takin' my time now, I worked open the door's lock and limped outside, carrying my baby and the sickle. Faint moonlight shown on the dead grass, on the baby, and on me. I saw my shadow layin' out before me, and it wasn't me. It was a huge, tall, long armed-creature with a sickle in its hand.

But that weren't bad.

'Cause I liked it.

I understood it. I was it.

My baby coughed and looked at me, all knowing-like.

Hell, we're in this together, I thought, and gave my baby a little nick on the arm with the blade. He chuckled.

"Cut cut cut cut," I heard the sickle whisper.

"Cut cut cut cut," I said.

"Cut cut cut cut," my baby said.

And now, the shadow on the ground was of a huge creature with long spider arms holding a smaller creature with long spider arms. It looked like what an audience might see when lights in the back of stage curtains cast silhouettes of a ventriloquist and his dummy right before their act.

And what an act there was gonna be.

Mama made me get rid of my first baby. Jeff dumped me. My sisters was little shits. Pete was an irresponsible asshole. These were the starters. My baby would have other ideas, too. We could talk about it as we went home. We could discuss it with the voice that chittered inside the sickle.

The world didn't stink no more. It smelled like blood and power.

It smelled real sweet.

Dust Cover

She wouldn't come out. But she smiled at me, with one colorless eye pressed to the gap in the doorway, her nose nearly hanging itself on the links of the chain-lock. She was pleased, and I could hear her grainy hands clapping together behind the wood.

"You'll love it," she said. "It's so homey and warm, like mine. It won't be any time before you'll swear you'll never live anywhere else."

I clucked my tongue, quietly though, so she wouldn't hear. It wouldn't do for her to sense my impatience. But I was impatient, and a bit confused. Mrs. Lacey had refused to show me the apartment herself. She wouldn't even step out to check me over, but had instead, poked the key through the crack and said to go on up. I had nodded, waiting, but she simply grinned like a tooth-bare Cheshire cat. And I had to go up by myself.

It didn't take long to look at the dusty apartment with its kitchen, bathroom, sleep-in living room, and houseplants. And it didn't take long to make a decision, either. It was January, and empty rentals near campus were at a premium. I needed the apartment. It was here or nowhere. So I pushed back my apprehension, and went to tell Mrs. Lacey that she had a new tenant.

"Good!" she said. Then she laughed, eyes alternating at the opening. "This is good! I hope you like plants. A little place like that needs living things, don't you think? You'll care for them, won't you?"

I nodded, thinking, *Hell, she's paying water and utilities, anyway, so I can handle it.*

She asked when I would be moving in. I said I'd be back within the week with my things.

I returned Saturday evening, laden with a suitcase, typewriter, and two bags of groceries. Mrs. Lacey's door opened to the length of the chain as I put my foot on the bottom step.

"What'cha got there?" she asked. One aged, Cyclops-eye blinked at the hall light.

"Stuff," I answered, wondering if this nosy welcome would become a habit. "And it's very heavy," I added, excusing myself; then I climbed the stairs, unlocked the apartment door, and went in.

The place was dark; the shades had been pulled against the glaring winter sun. But in spite of it, I could see the difference.

"Jeez," I said, flipping on the light. The dust, which I remembered as a thin film, was now a dense layer, carpeting everything from linoleum to potted fushia. I trekked across the floor to the kitchen table and plopped the grocery bags down. Dust fluttered.

I shook my head. Mrs. Lacey could have at least cleaned up before I moved in. It was disgusting.

I pulled up the shades. Light and dust tumbled like disturbed insects. I waved a hand before my face, coughing. Pledge wasn't going to take care of this mess. Reluctantly, I went back downstairs, ready to deal.

"It's unbelievable," I told her as her face appeared at the crack. "Have you been up there lately? Somebody needs to get a garden hose and rinse the place down."

Mrs. Lacey's powder-grey eye widened. "Oh, no, you probably wouldn't want to do that. Could run down through the floor, you know, ruin the floors, furniture, everything."

"Then how about a cleaning service? You can't really expect me to take the apartment as it is — "

"Oh, yes," she said.

I hesitated. "Oh yes, what?"

"Oh yes," she repeated, still smiling. "You must take it as it is, or not take it at all."

I stared at her, dumbfounded. "That makes no sense."

Mrs. Lacey just smiled.

Damn. Guess the cleaning will be on me, then. A full day at the very least, getting rid of the freaking dust.

"Well," I finally managed, "I guess I best go get settled then."

"Fine," she said, her fingers working through the crack and patting my arm. "Make yourself at home. We're glad you're here."

"Who's we?"

Mrs. Lacey shut the door, and as it was closing I thought I saw a large piece of dust float down and attach itself to her eyebrow.

I brought the rest of my belongings up from the car, and then collected several old towels and the Pledge. The living room would be first; it was the worst. I sprayed the corner of a towel and pressed it to the windowsill.

I knew it was the poor lighting, although I'll admit I flinched and my hand jerked away a fraction. But no, I told myself sternly as I put the edge of the towel back on the sill. Surely, it was the light or the air stirring through the window casing. Again, I pushed the towel to the left. And again, I stopped cold.

That's impossible, I thought.

It had looked as though the dust had moved away from the towel, not as a breeze might move it, but purposefully, as if it were rolling or crawling away.

"Totally impossible," I said aloud. It was the result of the greyed sunlight filtering through the dust-thickened window glass. I picked up the can of Pledge and sprayed the dust directly. It foamed and hissed, bubbles popping and glistening, then sank back into a flat, muddy liquid with what sounded like a sigh.

"That's some powerful stuff," I said, wondering if I'd gotten industrial strength spray instead of regular. I wiped the sill clean, then climbed on the radiator, pushed the curtains apart, knocking dusty cobwebs from their perch, and sprayed the top window. The brown foam blistered, then ran thin and wet.

It took seven towels and three hours to remove the crust from the apartment. The plants were the biggest challenge. The dust was practically embedded in the leaves; only the sharp edge of my fingernail file could scrape them clean.

The towels were rinsed in the bathtub, the sludge whirl-pooling, seeming to struggle, and then disappearing down the drain. I hung them on the rod, went into the living room, and flung myself down on the sofa with the newest *People* magazine and my favorite crocheted afghan.

I dozed, though I don't know how long.

My eyes opened to the ceiling tiles above me, draped with soft strings of cobwebs. I blinked, rubbed my eyes, and stared at the tiles. The cobwebs, which had been cleaned away (how long ago? how long had I slept?) were swaying slowly, thick, fuzzy, mocking fingers, dust clinging to them like pollen to bee legs. As I watched, a strand broke from the tiles and floated purposefully away. I turned on my side, following the strand. It drifted to the living room window.

My heart flipped.

The window was obliterated with dust.

"Damn," I hissed, rolling from the couch and cracking my knee on the floor. Not only was the window covered, but the drapes, walls, and radiator. I clambered to my feet, mouth hanging open like a broken drawer. A cobweb dropped from the ceiling onto my tongue. I spat it out in disgust. Several more dusty swirls flew past me on their way to the window. *What is this shit?* I thought. *Can dust migrate? Of course not. Is my mind going?*

I went into the kitchen. There had to be a breeze, a draft somewhere. This crap was blowing from somewhere and destroying all my hours of hard labor. I moved my hands around, feeling. There was nothing. I went back into the living room and checked the wall vent, thinking surely it must be the culprit. But there was nothing, no draft, not even the slightest hint of movement.

Dust in the wall, that had to be it. Heat kicks on and blows it out. Mrs. Lacey should have told me. Maybe she doesn't know.

Maybe.

Seconds later, I was bouncing my fist off her door.

"What's that?" came a croaking, demanding voice.

"I need to talk to you."

"It's late, you know. I'm going to bed."

"We need to talk now. I've got a problem in my apartment."

"What's that?"

"A problem with the vent."

Mrs. Lacey smiled.

"What's with the smile? Mrs. Lacey, I'm being serious. There's a problem. The vent is blowing crap all over the apartment."

"I caulked the windows in October."

"No, it's the vent. Would you please just open the door?"

"Just a minute." There was a shuffling, and then her door cracked open.

"What's this now?" she asked, a white tangle of hair hanging in her eye like a cobweb.

"The kitchen vent," I said. "Dirt's blowing in from the vent."

"Dirt?"

"Whatever you want to call it. It must be in the walls or something. I worked hours cleaning up. Now it's worse than ever."

"Vent's blowing dust." She was nodding, touching her lip with her bony finger.

"Yes."

"Push a chair against it," she said. "You got a chair?"

"Of course."

"Cover it with a chair. No problem."

"But I've still got this mess."

Mrs. Lacey's smile widened.

I sighed angrily. It was useless. Tomorrow, we would have a face-to-face sit down to come up with a solution.

"Good night, Mrs. Lacey," I said.

"Night," she said, and closed the door.

I went back to my apartment, shoved the chair in front of the vent, and curled up on the couch. And fell into a restless sleep.

In my dreams, I was staring where the vent's steel webbing had been punched out, leaving a black, gaping hole in the wall. I climbed from the couch, curious and frightened. There was something in that hole, something deep in the darkness, pulling me to it, my arms reaching out, my legs on fire with the adrenalin of fear. I had to look. I had to see. My hands groped ahead of me, now in the cool air, now before the vent hole, now reaching out, reaching in, down.

It rushed past my fingers like million moth wings, and hit my face with the force of a padded sledgehammer. I was slammed backward, my breath sucked from my throat, a cottony vise wrapping about my face, squeezing, crushing inward. I clawed at it. I tried to scream.

"Help me!" I screamed, sitting bolt upright. My hands went instantly to my face, to assure me that indeed I had been dreaming, and I clawed away something heavy, soft, and matted.

It was a thick clump of dust.

"What is this?!"

The clump squealed, squirmed, and jumped from my hand. I leapt up, landing shin-deep in a sea of filth, fell to my knees, and came up gagging.

Waves of dust swelled and battered my legs like living quicksand. I stumbled toward the door, tore my coat from the wall hook, and yanked the door open. As I squeezed through the opening, my eyes registered a final image within the apartment – the easy chair on its side, the dust crawling cheerfully from the deep black vent hole.

I raced down the stairs and jumped from the porch into the newly fallen snow on the yard, panting, trying not to think. Grey shadows flickered about my feet.

I heard Mrs. Lacey at her window, pounding the glass, yelling at me. "No, no! You can't go! It needs people! It needs living things, don't you understand? I can't be the only one to care, there's got to be someone else. I thought you would understand!"

I glanced toward the house, toward Mrs. Lacey at window, toward the sight that now had me transfixed and horrified. Her hair was a net of dust; her nightclothes were powdered grey; strings of spitty webs hung from her lips. Behind her, like a massive white backdrop, was the dust, motionless under its own weight, only the top grains shifting like sand on a dune.

"Don't go!" she cried. "Give us a chance!"

When I made it to the safety of my car, I locked the door behind me and rested my head on the steering wheel. My brain was reeling, my heart slamming into my ribs. *Impassible*, I thought. *Impossible.* I found the keys in my jacket pocket, and with sighted fingers, jammed them in the ignition.

Then something moved on the windshield. Something fine and white and powdery.

Snow. It had to be snow.

I turned on the wipers, knocking it away.

I kept the wipers going all the way back to campus.

Pisspot Bay

"No, of course. We don't torture people in America. And people who make that claim just don't know anything about our country."—President George W. Bush to the Australian Press, October 18th, 2003.

Andy had been caught in the sweep. It happened so fast, he first thought it was a gag, something rigged up by that doofus Stephen whose dad owned the farm, something Stephen would have thought was really funny. But it wasn't so funny when all was said and done.

The party had been going on, people were dancing, cussing, laughing in the paddock and in the hot, dusty barn with the windows and doors thrown open. The beer was flowing heavy and fast as river water in spring. There were older girls there, too, from the community college up the road. College girls at a high school graduation bash was, well, heaven on earth with their tight jeans and halter tops and coolers filled with exotic beers none of the Lee High School grads had ever heard of before.

Strings of lights hung around the inside of the barn, making Christmas out of June. Heavy metal and rap music played on a battery-powered boom box, competing off and on with the throw-together band in the first stall, trying to get their amps to heat up but having a hard time with the irregular current that powered the lights in the barn.

There were thirty-some kids, laughing and drinking and taking off to the field to smoke their pot because, while there might not have been a lot of rules they respected, everybody knew it was fucking pathetic to smoke in a barn. Stephen's Dad made a living as a farmer; Stephen's Dad had said, "Sure, boys, throw yourselves a party in the barn, you deserve it," so nobody was going to take advantage of that and put Stephen's Dad's barn or his livelihood in danger.

They were good like that.

But then around 3 a.m. came the sweep. Blue and red lights in the distance, rumbling through the darkness up the long, pocked driveway from the main road, chasing down the barn like hounds after a raccoon. At first some of the kids thought a thunderstorm was coming up, what with the noise and the flashing lights, but before they even had time to swallow their latest swigs, the Callington County sheriff cars had slammed on their brakes beside the paddock, spraying straw dust and gnats, and were out with guns pointing.

"What the –?" began Stephen, but an officer shouted, "Everyone, freeze! Don't move a muscle!" and most everyone outside in the paddock and standing just inside the open barn door froze, except for two kids who were really drunk and fell off the fence railing they'd been trying to walk. They lay there, laughing in the dirt.

Andy was standing in the doorway between Stephen and a really cute brown-haired college girl named Erin. They'd been sipping on Sheepshead Stouts and talking about next year. Stephen explained how he was going to work with his dad. Andy, feeling no pain with the help of several bottles of stout, claimed he'd been accepted into the state university but was thinking it might be better to work a year before taking on another four years of school. This was a lie. Andy had okay grades but hadn't even applied to a college because his father was in the pen down in Mecklenburg and his mother could barely afford to pay for the rental house in which they lived. But Andy said it to impress Erin, and Stephen didn't contradict him. Andy was starting to think Erin liked him – that maybe he was only eighteen but that was just two years younger than her, and what was two years, anyway – when the police crashed the party.

Andy recognized one of the deputies. His name was Conrad Anthony, and he'd graduated from Andy's high school three years earlier. The rest of the deputies he didn't know. *What the hell is going on?* Andy thought.

"What the hell is going on?" Andy asked, and Conrad shouted, "Shut up, Andy! Freeze means your vocal cords, too!"

Andy said nothing more. Beside him, Erin was breathing rapidly and saying under her breath, "Oh, God, my mom's going to fucking kill me." Andy knew they were in trouble, all of them except the 21-year-olds maybe, but then maybe them, too, for contributing. Stephen boldly clutched his beer in plain view, his jaws tight.

This was going to go down bad. They'd all get arrested, they'd get booked. There'd be bail to pay and then fines all around and some sort of community service. Andy's mom didn't have the money for bail, and with his new job delivering beds and sofas from Howe's Furniture Store, he sure as hell didn't have time for any goddamned community service.

Within ten minutes, all the partiers were separated from each other, standing like scarecrows in the ass-scratchy field, some swearing angrily, others mute, the lights from the cruisers trained on them like spotlighted off-season deer. Each partier was questioned individually, voices kept low so no one else could hear the conversations.

Andy shivered in the hot Virginia breeze. He'd never been questioned by police before. What was he supposed to say, or not say? Would they have to read him his rights to talk to him? Was he supposed to admit to Erin providing booze, or should he lie to keep her out of trouble? And what if she admitted to buying it and he was caught in a lie? His chest hurt; it felt like there were spiders on his neck.

Then it was his turn. Two of the deputies, men he did not know, strolled up to him. Their faces were shadowed, but he knew they weren't smiling.

"Hey," said Andy. "What's up, man? Somebody steal a cow or kill a goat? Kiddin'. What's got you so—"

And without a word, cuffs were slapped roughly onto Andy's wrists and he was thrown into the back of a cruiser. As two officers climbed into the front of the car and closed their doors, the one in the passenger's seat glared back at

Andy and through the bullet-proof glass said, "You have the right to remain silent, you have the right to have an attorney present during questioning."

#

The questioning took place in the sheriff's department, a fifteen-mile drive from Stephen's farm and in the center of Greeneville, the nearest town. Andy didn't know if he was the only one arrested, or just the first one.

He sat, waiting, in a small room on the second floor. There were three rusty chairs, a small table, a couple of fading, curling posters on the wall showing sites around "Beautiful, Bountiful Virginia," a footed radiator, and a single window that faced out to a narrow alley and the brick side of Nation's Bank across the alley. It was morning, a bright and sunny day as far as Andy could tell. He had been in that little room for a couple hours. The two deputies who had arrested him had talked to him off and on, and he knew why he was there.

They said he'd planted a bomb.

Someone had called from Stephen's house during the party, and said they'd heard Andy bragging that he'd planted a bomb in the middle of town, a bomb set to go off at 6:52 p.m. the following day to commemorate the anniversary of the date and time when Andy's father had been found guilty of murder five years earlier. The caller had said that Andy knew his father was guilty of the killing but that it was self-defense, and that Andy was enraged that his father was treated like shit throughout the trial and then treated worse down in Mecklenburg's super max prison. Andy wanted somebody to suffer the way his father was suffering.

The initial questioning had been relaxed, almost friendly. When Andy heard the charges, he laughed incredulously and said he'd never done such a thing and couldn't guess who would want to get him in trouble like that. Inside, his guts twitched like a hooked fish on a lake bank and his mind spun with the booze he'd drunk, but he was proud to keep himself calm on the outside.

Who the hell would say something like that about him? he wanted to know. Who hated him that much? Or who was insane enough to play that kind of fucked-up prank? The deputies didn't know, and they smiled along with him.

Andy swore his innocence. The two deputies listened and nodded. They asked him if he wanted a Coke and he said no, though his mouth was dry. Conrad came in for a few minutes and they backed and forthed about ole Lee High, then Conrad left again. It was hot in the room, and Andy asked if they could open the window but they said no, it wasn't that hot. They said Andy probably was feeling it more since he was still intoxicated. They said if they opened the window, flies would come in, and flies irritated the sheriff almost as much as criminals.

The deputies asked Andy about his home life. Andy didn't want to talk about it but he did, because he wanted to make them happy, make them like him, make them know he wasn't his father's son, really, he was a nice guy. He told the officers his mother worked at the Dollar General, cashiering, doing inventory, that kind of thing. His younger brother was in middle school, a goofy little kid who liked band better than football. His family had gone bankrupt a couple years back when Andy's father went to prison, but otherwise was doing okay. No, Andy didn't hate anybody and nobody that he knew of hated him. What did Andy think of those bombings he'd seen on TV, over in the Middle East and Europe? Andy said they were stupid. What did Andy think of the planes crashing into the World Trade Towers and the Pentagon? Of ISIS terrorizing and bombing and killing innocent people? Andy said they were stupid, too.

Andy thought about asking for a lawyer but he watched TV and knew how once you asked for a lawyer, they thought you were guilty. They no longer questioned you but threw you in a cell. He didn't want to get booked and go in a cell. It would all be cleared up real soon, so he would hang tight. Soon, whoever had made the call would confess his prank.

The deputies offered Andy something to eat and he said no. Then they said they would wait to talk to him more after he'd sobered up. Andy guessed that made sense, so he leaned back in the chair and closed his eyes, hoping it wouldn't take long. The world spun and he felt like throwing up, so he opened his eyes again.

Now, for the first time since being brought to the station, he was alone. Well, he didn't really think he was totally alone. There was a two-way mirror on the wall. He knew that someone was always watching from behind that glass. Waiting for him to pick his nose or scratch his ass or try to hang himself with his shoestrings or something.

The sun was up and it was damned hot in the room. The radiator hissed softly as if it had been turned on. Andy wiped sweat from his forehead and wished he'd gone for that Coke. When they came back, he'd ask them for one and then ask when he would get to go home. By now, certainly, the truth had come out. Any minute now, they'd come and say go home. It was a joke, a hideous joke and if he found out who did it he'd beat the shit out of him, but still a joke. Andy didn't know explosives from a hole in the roof. Well, he blew up some toy trucks and soldiers with leftover Fourth of July fireworks back when he was thirteen. That was fun. But it wasn't a bomb.

There was no clock on the wall and Andy didn't have a watch or cell phone. He wondered what time it was. His back hurt from the chair. Wasn't he allowed a phone call? His head was clearing, and he knew he was supposed to be able to call somebody. He'd call his mom. What would he tell her?

A janitor came into the room, an old man with a blue jump suit and squinty eyes. He said they needed the chairs in the other room, and told Andy to stand up. Andy did, and the janitor stacked the three chairs and took them out. Andy called after him, "I think that radiator's busted, it's pouring hot air," but the janitor didn't say anymore, and he shut the door behind him. Andy stood by the wall, and then sat on the table. He wiped the sweat from his brow and forearms.

Conrad came in about a half hour later with Sheriff Bateman. Bateman crossed his arms and said, "Don't sit on the table, son."

Andy stood up. He thought about sitting on the floor but guessed that might be a bad idea, as unhappy as the sheriff looked.

Bateman said, "Well, the bomb isn't in our building, and it isn't in the courthouse."

"That's good," said Andy.

"I wonder where it is?"

"I'm really tired," said Andy. "It's awful hot in here. I got to go home before my mother thinks somebody killed me or something."

Bateman looked at Conrad then at Andy. He said, "Where's the bomb? We don't have time to mess with you. We need to know. You tell us, it'll go easier, you know it will."

"What?" Andy asked.

"You don't want to hurt anybody. We don't want anybody to get hurt. Let's work together. We know you're upset about your dad, but come clean and it'll go easier."

"What?"

"Talk now, Andy. We can get the state police in here, or the FBI if we have to, and we will, believe me. You know how much harder they'll be on you? Now, where's the bomb?"

"There isn't a bomb."

"We think there is."

"Well, then somebody else did it, not me."

"You got motive, Andy. We trust the caller. We believe he told us the truth."

"I didn't plant a bomb. I don't know anything at all about bombs."

"Where is it, Andy?"

"I didn't plant a bomb!"

"We found bomb-making materials in your shed at home."

"You did not!"

Bateman nodded.

Did the sheriff find bomb-making stuff? What's bomb-making stuff?

Andy said, "What did you find?"

"You know very well what we found."

What did they find? Some kind of fertilizer or something? Do we have that at home? Mom raises vegetables in the summer. Is that the fertilizer they found? Are they lying? Police are allowed to lie, I know that. Are they lying?

"I want a lawyer," Andy said. He didn't mean to say it, but it came out, anyway. He was no longer holding it together on the outside. His hands were shaking madly and his shoulders jumped with every word.

"Hmm. Okay." The sheriff went quiet for a moment, staring out the window. On his forehead, Andy could see sweat beads gathering then rolling. "We'll do that. You got a name? A lawyer?"

"No," said Andy. "I need one, though. I can't afford one."

"Okay. I'll put in a call to the public defender. Might be a while."

"How long?"

Bateman shrugged. "Just hold tight there, Andy."

"I need to call my mom."

Bateman said, "All our lines are busy right now, but as soon as one opens up we'll put you through. That okay with you? Got any problems with that?"

"Yes," said Andy. "I mean no."

Then Bateman came right up to him, nose to sweaty nose, and said evenly, "You admire those terrorists, Andy? You like their power, the way they teach the world a lesson, don't you?" Spit flew from the sheriff's mouth onto Andy's face, but Andy didn't move to wipe it away. "You want to be just like them, to kill people when you don't like something. Following in your daddy's footsteps, huh, but you're going to take it a lot further than he did, huh?"

"What? No!" said Andy. He knew the sheriff wasn't supposed to ask him anything else since he requested a lawyer. But then the sheriff blew a puff of air through his teeth and said, "Just rhetorical, Andy. I know you can't answer me now, now you begged for a lawyer. Fuckin' redneck terrorist."

Bateman glared at Andy a long moment. Then he turned to Conrad. "Here's your little schoolmate, trying to kill people in town 'cause his murderin' daddy doesn't get cable TV down the prison."

Andy saw that Conrad was unsure of what to do or say. Conrad and Andy were on the basketball team together one year. He wondered if Conrad believed the lie.

"If this bastard's your friend," Bateman told Conrad, "then warn him that the FBI's been called. They're on their way. It won't be pretty, lawyer or not. This isn't some purse-snatching or B-and-E. This is a whole other ballgame. We're livin' in a whole different world from a couple years ago. And we don't have time to pussyfoot around threats like the one he's made."

Bateman stormed out and slammed the door.

Andy said, "Con, I didn't do anything! You know me!"

"Phone call said you did, Andy. Said you were high by the time you got to the party, stoned on something. Said you were all riled about your mom being treated like shit because of your dad being in prison."

"She *is* treated like shit," said Andy. "Me, too, sometimes, and my brother. But that doesn't mean I'd –"

"Were you high when you got to the party? Just between you and me, I ain't asking as a deputy, okay?"

"Well," said Andy. He'd smoked pot before going to Stephen's farm, half a joint. When he got to the farm at seven, Stephen and a couple other guys were snorting in one of the stalls and offered Andy some. Andy thought about it; fuck, it was a graduation party and time to celebrate. Did he snort? Maybe he did and didn't remember. No, he remembered not going for it. "No, I wasn't high. Well, maybe a little but I knew what I was doing."

"Then you started drinking," said Conrad.

"Some."

"You remember everything you did before the officers got there?"

"Sure."

"You didn't pass out, early in the night, then get woken up around eleven and rejoin the party?"

Did I? "Fuck, Conrad, it's killer hot in here. Can we talk somewhere else? I've been in here hours. I feel sick."

"No."

"I don't remember if I passed out. I'm pretty sure I didn't."

"If you passed out, you might not remember what you said, Andy. People do all sorts of stuff when they're drunk, then they pass out and forget what they did. Some guys even married girls when they were drunk, then afterwards swore they never saw the woman in their whole life."

Did I? Did I get drunk and make some fucking threat about bombing a building in town?

"Who called? Who said I made the threat?"

"Can't tell you."

"Why not?"

"It's confidential. What if you found out who told us, got mad, and threatened to kill him, too?"

"I don't kill people!"

A pager on Conrad's hip beeped. He said, "Got to go. Think about it, Andy. It'll go easier if you just own up."

Conrad left the room. Andy paced back and forth. The heat was almost unbearable, and his legs threatened to give way beneath him. Blackness gnawed at the edge of his vision. His stomach cramped viciously. He pounded on the door. "Let me out! I'm sick! I'm going to faint!"

No one responded. He dropped down and tried to breathe cooler air through the space beneath the door. He shouted from the floor, "Help me, I'm sick!"

A moment later, the door was thrown open, whacking Andy in the head and splitting the skin of his scalp. He clutched the door and pulled himself slowly to his feet, warm blood trickling toward his cheek. A deputy he didn't know scowled at him. "I don't feel good . . ." Andy began.

"I'll show you the bathroom," the deputy said.

Already, the cooler air coming in from the hallway started to ease his dizziness. "Is my lawyer here?"

"Not yet."

"And I got a call to make."

"All the phones are still busy."

"Still? After all this time?"

"The phones are busy."

#

The bathroom was in the basement. Andy guessed there were nicer ones for the officers and for visitors to the department, but this one was down near the holding cells, at the back of the building. There were no windows at all in the room, just a vent near the ceiling. One stall housed a john; two hard water-stained urinals clutched the cinderblock walls. The floor was wet and warped. But it wasn't hot, for which Andy was grateful.

The deputy who'd taken him to the restroom didn't go in with him. Andy thought that was odd, but maybe hopeful. Maybe they were really starting to doubt his guilt and so didn't think he needed a babysitter. *How would I escape from here, anyway?* he thought, looking around. *Crawl through the toilet?* He finished taking a whiz, zipped up, and then sipped water from the faucet. He felt better, though not good. His stomach still hurt like hell.

The door opened and a large man came in. He was an inmate, one Andy had seen in a holding cell as he'd walked past. The man was unevenly tan and splotched, with several loose hairs on his head and a nose that looked like it had been broken several times. He smelled like old sweat. He leaned back against the door. "Hey, fella," he said.

Andy's heart kicked. "I'm through in here. Let me out and you can have the place to yourself, okay?"

"You sure is nothin'," chuckled the big man. "Big mouth, little man, huh?"

"Just move over and I'll get out of your way."

"Welcome to Pisspot Bay," said the man. "Like it in here?"

Oh shit what's this?

"You ever watch the news?" asked the man. He scratched his neck, leaving long red lines on the skin with his irregular, chipped nails. "They got suspects down Guantanamo Bay and over in Afghanistan and Iraq, some of those Arab fucks who threaten America, threaten to bomb us and shit. Know about them?"

"I guess."

"Those terrorists don't want to talk, you don't want to talk."

"Let me out of here."

"But you got to talk," said the man. "Welcome to Pisspot Bay, our own little detention center, boy. And you are going to talk. We ain't gonna let you get away with hurting other people. We gotta get to the truth. I ain't gonna do nothing they ain't doin' for national security. Call it 'stress and duress.' So suck it up or give it up."

Andy screamed at the top of his lungs, "Get me out of here! Somebody get me out!"

He knew they heard him, beyond that stinking bathroom. But no one came to the door.

#

"That's all I wanted," said the big man. "Just that, no big deal, right? Now, say it one more time." He patted Andy on the head.

"I . . . planted a bomb."

"And where is it?"

"It's in the school...in Lee High School."

Andy remembered planting the bomb. Not clearly, but as in a hazy dream. He made it in his shed at home, and hid it in the gymnasium where he used to play basketball on the varsity team. He didn't recall how he made the bomb, or actually taking it to the school, but that wasn't the important thing. He was angry that his father was treated like crap and so was the rest of his family. He wanted to get back at the community so he made a bomb. He had confessed. Things would be better for him now, the big man promised.

The big man helped Andy to his feet, but his legs would not lock beneath him. He'd been forced to crouch beside the urinals for over an hour, with his hands bound behind his back. His legs and feet were numb. While Andy was crouching, the man had put towels over Andy's face then poured water over them time and time again.

"This doesn't really hurt you," the man had explained. "It will just help you remember."

Andy had gagged and thrashed and choked, certain he was drowning. He felt close to passing out several times, and threw up twice. The man only laughed and said, "Just cleanin' out the gunk is all. You'll be fine once you fess up."

And now the session was over. Andy held on to the big man as the feeling drained back into his legs. He whimpered and then he cried. With the return of blood came searing, knife-like pains sawing into the muscles of his thighs and calves.

"Oh, shut up, you little baby," said the man, almost affectionately. "You'll be fine in a while. Flex your feet and your calves. See? There you go. And if you decide you didn't plant the bomb, if you change your mind or you forget what you did, we can come back in here and go through this all again. How's that sound?"

The man opened the bathroom door and led Andy, hobbling, into the basement hallway. The deputy who had brought him down was sitting in a folding chair not five feet from the bathroom door, chatting with a jail guard and chewing gum.

Andy didn't ask why he'd ignored the screams in the bathroom. It didn't really matter now, did it? He was a criminal; he'd done a terrible thing. Now they could take care of the terrible thing and no one would get hurt. The deputy helped Andy down the hall and up the steps as the big man was given some cigarettes and chocolate from the guard and put back inside his cell.

Andy blinked in the bright afternoon light that poured through the glass in the front door. He was told to sit on one of the benches by the front desk, and he did so, gratefully. Did he still get a phone call? Had the lawyer arrived? He would tell them whatever they needed to know. He would not go back to Pisspot Bay.

An hour passed, an hour and a half, and then Conrad Anthony came to see him in the hallway.

"Your lawyer's here, Andy. Let's talk."

Andy was ushered into the interrogation room where he'd first been brought so many hours ago. The radiator was off. The window was open and fresh air coursed through, smelling of a small-town summer. The chairs were back in the room. Andy dropped into one of them and put his hands in his hair.

Across the table sat a man with bushy gray beard. He said, "Son, my name is George Parker. I'm your attorney."

"I did it," whispered Andy. "Find it and get rid of it. It's in the gym at school."

Parker's face clouded. "You are confessing? We haven't even talked yet."

Andy wiped dried tears from his face, feeling as though new ones were very close behind. "Yeah. Find it. Get it out. I never wanted to hurt anyone, really. Do I get it better now, for telling the truth? Please? Please?"

#

There was no bomb in Lee High School's gymnasium, or anywhere else. The bomb squad and their sniffing dogs searched every inch of the school, as well as the buildings surrounding it. There was nothing.

The boy who had called the sheriff's department admitted early in the afternoon to lying to get Andy in trouble. He said he didn't know it would go that far, but that Andy was a pompous son-of-a-bitch who should know his place, what with a killer father and all. "Andy needed to come down a peg," the boy said. The boy would be fined for a false report, but he could afford it, his father owned the Ford car dealership in Greeneville.

Andy's mother came to pick him up at six-fifteen that evening, furious that he hadn't called and relieved that he was all right. At home, there was a letter from his father waiting, and a cold Coke, and a *Motor Sports* magazine his mother had brought Andy from the store.

Sarah, In the Attic

Sarah would not be told no. Oh, no not at all. There had never been a time in her beautiful life that she had been rejected, denied, or corrected.

Nope.

Newly wed to the wealthy, soft-spoken Henry Blauer-Bart, Sarah immediately took over the house following their whirlwind courtship and exotic, extended honeymoon.

When Henry told Sarah the oak-paneled room in the east wing was his private man cave, she promptly had all his heavy furniture replaced with white wicker and pink pillows. When he explained how he enjoyed playing pool with his friends in the billiard room, she immediately had the pool table taken out and put mirrors on the wall and mats on the floor so she could do her morning yoga. When he explained that a clean bedroom was important for his peace of mind at the end of the day, she made a point of leaving her towels and lingerie and shoes all over the floor. When he put the portrait of his former, deceased wife, Colleen away in a closet, Sarah had brought it back out again and had hung it over the bed, explaining, "This is so she can see who is enjoying her man now!" When Henry told her the attic was not a safe place to explore, she waited until he'd gone out on the lake in his boat to pull down the folding stairs and climb right up into it.

Yep.

The attic had only one light, turned on by the pull of a string. Sarah winked in the dim light and peered around to see a number of trunks scattered about. Each trunk had a name on it. "Rachel." "Mary." "Donna." "Colleen."

Sarah wrinkled her brow. "Oh, seriously now. How many wives has Henry had? And he didn't kill them all and put their bodies up here in the attic, did he?"

She opened the trunk marked, "Colleen," to find a lovely set of elegant dresses, blouses, and capes folded neatly within.

"Pretty! I will have these as my own!" exclaimed Sarah. She stepped out of her sweater and slacks and slipped on one of Colleen's lacy gowns.

And then the dress began to squeeze. It grew tighter and tighter as Sarah gasped, writhed and stumbled. Her face turned purple and her eyes popped.

"Bitch," said the gown as Sarah went down. "Each new wife wants what ain't hers, what she don't deserve. Nobody learns lessons 'round here. Bye bye, baby."

Oops.

Henry Blauer-Bart found Sarah in the attic, shook his head. He threw her body into the lake, put her clothes in a new trunk labeled "Sarah," and went out on the town.

I really should rethink what I want in a wife, he thought as he watched the young women in the bar. A buxom brunette came flouncing over and he bought her a drink.

Oh, well.

ꝗ Have a Little Shadow

Claire stood still, naked, listening. The room was silent except for the humming of the air-conditioning and the pulsing blood behind her ears.

Maybe I've outrun them this time. Maybe I've outsmarted them.

She stepped closer to the room's center, because if they were anywhere they would be hiding in the little slices of shadow beneath the bedframe and mattress that she had stood on end and shoved against the closet door. She knew their tiny, clicking sounds and their distorted, tiny faces. Over the past two weeks they had made themselves known to her quite clearly. There were also times that they lay low and kept quiet. Maybe they were in the motel room with her, waiting. Waiting for her to let down her guard.

She knelt on the sticky carpet and squinted at the base of the mattress and frame. The shadows were as thin as pencil lines, but that didn't matter. They could bend to the shape and size of the darkness.

"Are you here?" she whispered. There was no answer, none of the typical, hissing whispers her desperate questions had usually brought about, so she thought she might truly have left them behind for the time being.

Please, I need rest!

Claire stood again, took in a deep breath, and let her gaze move about the bare interior of her motel room. The nightstand and television on its small table had been wheeled into the bathroom. Claire had closed the door then lined the crack with several washcloths. She didn't use a towel because towels were bulkier and cast more of a shadow. The curtains had been taken down and shoved into the bathtub. Unfortunately, of course, the bed hadn't fit.

Flashlights lay all around the floor, dozens of them, turned on and pointed in every possible direction. It was early morning and pale sunlight added its welcomed beam to that of the flashlights and overhead bulb. As long as there was no shadow around Claire, she was safe.

Outside were the sounds of families going and coming from the motel, children laughing, parents shouting, cars biting the gravel of the motel parking lot. Inside, there was only the sound of Claire's breathing, the rushing pulse in her head, and her whispered mantra.

"Surely goodness and mercy shall follow me all the days of my life." The words she spoke were no longer a prayer but a chant, a net of verbal protection thrown into the air to snare the things that kept after her.

She waited as the reverberation of her voice stilled and then spoke again, pivoting on her feet in a slow circle to watch all corners of the well-lit room in case there were shadows she'd not detected. "He makes me lie down in green pastures, he leads me beside the still water. Surely goodness and mercy shall follow me."

God's mercy and goodness had not been following her for the past two weeks. *They* had.

The motel room was unbearably cold. After repositioning the furniture last night, she'd seen the shadows inside the air-conditioning control box and had been afraid to reach in to turn it down. The tips of her ears beneath her close-cropped hair were freezing. Her arms shook against the cold.

Claire stepped closer to the window to peer outside. Her scratched white Escort sat in the slot marked for room #5. The car was out of gas and she was nearly out of money. It was a miracle she'd made it this far. Yet she wasn't sure she believed in miracles anymore. She had at one time. It had been in every fiber of her body to believe and to coast on the goodness of her God and the certainty of her mission.

But she wasn't certain anymore.

"Surely, goodness and mercy," she repeated. "Goodness and mercy shall follow me." She touched her lower lip with her fingers. They were sunburned and cracked, dry with fear and poor nutrition. She pushed the lip until she felt a trickle of salty blood. Salt, an essence of life. The Bible had said that whosoever followed the Light was the salt of the earth.

She had once understood the Light.

But she could not understand the shadows. None of this made any sense.

The name of the motel was "See Sea" but it was across the street from the beach and there was a high-rise built on the oceanfront, so the See Sea couldn't see squat. When Claire was a little girl, she and her family had spent many happy summers at this motel, and back then you could, indeed, see the sea. The sand dunes hadn't been scraped up artificially high and there had been a path through the sand and the sea oats that waved in the wind on either side. From your motel window you could watch the churning, foamy salt water and crashing waves, and it always made Claire feel peaceful.

Out on the parking lot today, a mother with three squirming children headed out toward the road. The woman wore sunglasses and a broad-brimmed sun hat that shaded her face in near-black. The kids flicked gravel at each other and whacked each other with rolled up towels. The mother didn't notice; her eyes were focused straight ahead, probably trying to figure out exactly how to get to the water around the massive, fenced property line of the high-rise.

Maybe I've really outrun them this time.

Claire had been traveling for many days, taking obscure roads to confuse them. But they didn't confuse easily.

Who are they? And why me? What have I done to deserve this torment? I've always done my best to do good! It's the evil who are supposed to be plagued and hunted!

Claire knelt in the protective circle of flashlights and prayed.

After an hour, her prayers unanswered, she checked her clothes with the flashlights and then donned them to venture outside in search of something to eat. All she had were six sweaty dollars in the front pocket of her shorts, with a few nickels and some lint. The last of her money had gone into the gas tank. She'd never been without before. She'd never been dirty before. She'd never experienced cravings. It was something others felt. God had never left her wanting, and now, she wanted.

I'm so hungry, she thought. *Let me find a place that serves cheap food.*

She walked over a mile, past the usual assortment of motels, hotels, and beach houses. Her feet grew sore and blistered. She was not used to walking. She was used to traveling by car, plane, taxi. It wasn't that she believed she was too good to walk, but people were always offering her rides and tickets and fares. It was their gift, and she felt it was her duty to accept.

Her eyelids fluttered against the brightness of the noon sun. She wondered how long until the little demons would crawl right up into the shadows of her lids. She could not shade her face, but this made her recognizable to the public. This made her all the more vulnerable.

What terrible act brings me to be food for devils? What have I done but that which I should have done?

Weariness and hunger caused her footsteps to miss a beat. She stumbled sideways and a car, whizzing past with its convertible top down and its interior stuff with teenagers, honked loudly. One occupant yelled, "Watch it, lady, or you'll be killed!" Laughter followed, howls of many decibels and in several keys, and then it faded as the car grew smaller and shimmered in the mirage of water on the road. In its retreating shadow, Claire saw sharp, grinning teeth.

Soon Claire reached the spot of town where shops, restaurants, and conference centers lined the street. There were stoplights here, and much traffic. Most of the gift shops were of the cheaper kind, selling inflatable rafts that would last a day before popping, Parnell Beach t-shirts, seashell animal creations, and saltwater taffy. The restaurants ran the spectrum from sandy, barefoot ice cream stands to expensive seafood establishments in which a man needed a tie and a woman needed a good pair of heels and a coifed hairdo.

Claire's own hair was straight and shaved close to prevent shadows on her head. Her shoes were cheap flip flops, open to the sun. She'd bought them soon after she'd escaped St. Anne's Mission in New York, following the first sighting of the creatures in the mission's basement. They had been inside a box of donated food, and she had nearly touched them as she'd reached for several cans.

"Tooooooooooo," they had called to her. And she had dropped the cans and run back upstairs.

Claire took a deep breath through her mouth, tasting the salt of the sea and the sand of the earth. She had not cried yet. They had been watching and following her for many days now, yet she had not cried.

A Dairy Queen Brazier sat on the ocean side of the street, with a line of wilted vacationers waiting their turn at the order window. Claire got behind the last girl and looked at the ground. The gravel was sparkling and hot with sunshine. She slipped one foot out of her flip flop and touched a rock with her toe. When she was little, she liked to run barefoot in the summer. She liked to jump into the waves and dig for tiny crabs with paper cups and bury her father in the sand.

The little girl in front of Claire turned around and grinned. She was missing her front teeth, like any normal seven-year-old. She said, "I'm getting a banana split. What are you getting?"

Claire felt her lips pull into a smile that she hoped appeared genuine. "I don't know yet."

"Get a banana split. They're best."

"I'm sure they are."

"Then get one."

"We'll see."

The little girl's face grew serious. She frowned with thought, wrapping one finger through a dark curl. *She knows me,* Claire thought, and so she looked away to end the conversation.

The line moved up a bit, gray traces of shadows flickering around the customers' feet in spite of the fact that the sun was directly overhead. Claire watched the shadows, ready to move should they produce monsters. Then she glanced in through the snack bar's open window at the menu – hot dogs, hamburgers, fish filets, chicken patties. She hadn't eaten meat since she was seventeen. She believed eating the flesh of fellow sentient creatures was a sin. French fries, onion rings. Terrible on the arteries but at least they came from plants.

Two more steps forward. A young couple, in love, strolled away from the order window, arms linked, each holding matching parfait glasses with swirls of chocolate, pineapple, and vanilla ice cream. Claire had had a boyfriend once. She had been twelve and he had been eleven. Joey Robinson. They'd held hands and played in the sprinkler and he even kissed her after supper one time before having to go home. But then, years later, God had called in His booming, joyless voice and everything had changed.

Glancing at the gravel again, Claire saw a small piece of rock within the shadow of a light pole tremble on its own, then roll over. Slowly, like something underneath was trying to get out. The hairs on Claire's arms stood at attention.

Several over pieces of gravel followed suit, rolling away from each other within the small space of the shadow, opening a small slash in the darkness. Claire saw their tiny eyes in that slash, unearthly eyes, starting up at her.

"Tooooooooooo," they said.

Claire gasped.

They winked at her and said again, "Tooooooooooo gooooooo...."

God, no! Leave me alone!

Claire jumped back, knocking down a small boy who'd been standing beside his father. The father cursed and demanded an apology as he pulled his son back up and the boy began to cry. Claire ran from the Dairy Queen and back out to the street.

On a corner, she clutched her head in her hands. *What wrong have I done? What terrible crime am I guilt of? I've done my best! I've lived for You!* She thought back, once again, on the life she'd lived for God.

As a senior in high school, Claire Cullen had fallen out of love with Joey and in love with Jesus. It hadn't been a slow, thought-out decision, but one of immediacy, like the blinding flashes one reads about in the Bible. One day she'd been picking out her prom dress and the next she had been taking all her fancy clothes to the Salvation Army for the needy, leaving herself only a few plain shirts and pairs of jeans. She'd graduated but did not go to college as her parents had hoped. Instead, she'd moved to inner city New York to help out at a homeless shelter. She'd only thought to be an assistant at the place, to help bathe and mop floors and cook, but there had been something the mission tenants loved about her. Her face, her gentle smile, her way with the word of God.

Soon, the shelter not only drew in the indigent to hear her talks, but the local merchants and ministers as well. The merchants, who had adamantly opposed the shelter because it scared off customers, found their hearts changed. Some offered jobs and spare rooms to the homeless. Minsters, who had thought bums deserved their bad lot because of drinking and drugs, opened their arms and welcomed the unwanted to church supper services.

Claire's fame grew and spread. She had never wanted to be a preacher. She believed herself unworthy. Like Moses, she'd though herself slow of speech. But it was a role given her, and the words flowed forth.

Talks at the city's social service commission meetings, speeches before the state legislature, and not long afterwards invitations to address Congress and to visit the White House. Her face made the major newspapers and magazines. Her impassioned and intelligent pleas on behave of the poor and displaced were declared brilliant, moving Democrat and Republicans alike to look again at the downtrodden with softened eyes and minds. Her face, simple and pretty, reminded the world of the late Princess Diana of Great Britain. Her hands had even wrought occasional and surprising miracles of healing. Not even Rush Limbaugh could find fault with Claire Cullen.

Claire. Dubbed "Mother Claire" by the *New York Times*. Twenty-seven years old. Young, blonde-haired, brown-eyed savior. Generator of billions for the needy in money, goods, medicines, and services. In the few years she had been in the limelight, the number of homeless children had gone down drastically. The numbers of drugged-out transients on the city streets had likewise diminished greatly. She was a success. Reluctantly, she hired a small staff to help her arrange talks, organize events, and get from place to place.

America was beautiful again. The country's consciousness had shifted to magnanimity and light had shown from sea to shining sea.

And then, they had appeared. In the shadow in the box of canned food in the mission basement. After her initial scare, Claire was sure what she'd seen was caused by weariness. She had left the mission and gone to visit her mother's farm in Pennsylvania for a week's vacation. But out in the field on a walk, beneath the small grove of trees she and Joey used to climb, she saw something in the shadows. Dreadful demon faces, staring at her. Speaking something low and threatening – "Toooooooo gooooo....."

"I decided I don't need this vacation," she'd told her publicist on the phone in her mother's kitchen. "I need to get back to work. I want to spend time at the DC mission. Please get me a plane ticket."

She'd flown to the capital city in order to work at one of the new missions that bore her name, "Mother Claire's Home for the Intellectually Disabled." She had hoped to scrub floors, cook some meals, and sit with some of the residents and play games. She wanted to be anonymous again. Fame was clearly messing with her sense of reality.

But her arrival in Dulles Airport was heralded and she spent the next few days, instead, in the Lincoln bedroom at the invitation of the president.

It was on the second night at the White House, while drifting off to sleep, that they came for her en masse, calling and crawling out from shadows cast by antique furniture and elegant corners. She'd grabbed her clothes, told the president she was needed elsewhere, and fled.

She'd been running and hiding ever since.

In the crack between two segments of concrete on the sandy sidewalk, deep where sunlight could not reach, she saw movement. Sharp-tipped fingers wiggling. Silvery eyes peering. Little mouths drooling.

"What is it?" she screamed at the walk. "Why have you come for me?"

Passersby made wide berths and gave her quick and disapproving glances. One tapped on her cell phone, perhaps calling for the police or an ambulance.

I know I sound insane! But they are real!

Sweat dripping from her forehead and nose, Claire went inside a small gift shop and stood beside the display of personalized key chains. The air from the vent overhead washed down and eased her skin. She caught a whiff of herself and realized she was beginning to stink. She had never smelled bad before. It was grossly humiliating.

"May I help you?"

It was the rashy-faced boy behind the cash register. He looked like he preferred Claire be anywhere but in the store.

Claire shook her head. "No, thank you."

But the boy came around from behind the counter and walked over. His expression shifted from disgust to inquisitiveness. "Hey," he said, "Hey, don't I know you?"

Claire hated to lie. Lying was wrong. "I don't know," she said honestly.

"What's your name?" He asked. His nose was wrinkled and she knew it was from her stench. But his curiosity had the best of him.

"Claire," she said.

"Claire what?"

"Do you sell sunscreen?"

"Of course." The boy scratched his cheek. "Hey, wait. Have you ever been on TV?"

"Quite often.

The boy tilted his head, studying her face, and then his face opened into one of the purest expressions of sheer joy she had ever seen. She knew he knew.

"Yes, yes!" he said. "It's you! Oh, bless me, please!"

The hope and expectation in his voice made Claire's stomach jump. She said, "Excuse me, I need to be going," and ran out past the key chains and the bathing suits and the sunscreen.

The beach was crowded. Umbrellas and beach chairs and towels littered the sand, and humans crawled the area like fleshy crabs. Even the herring gulls had a hard time finding landing spots.

The water washes away sin, Claire told herself. If she bathed in the sea, maybe the demons would stay clear of her. John the Baptist knew the power of water. So did Paul. So did the Lord Jesus.

She stepped out of her flip flops and began the trek across the sand toward the water. But beneath her feet, in her own growing shadow, she could feel them stirring. Beneath the sand, as the sun had begun its descent from the zenith of the sky, she could feel them struggling upward.

Sensed them watching. Heard their voices.

"Tooooooo goooood. Tooooo goooood, Claire."

She stifled a cry and began to walk faster.

"Don't yooooou know what yoooou've done?" they whispered. "Can't yoooou see into your shadow?"

"Stop, stop!" she answered, stumbling, righting herself. "You make no sense! Leave me alone!" She tried to run but the sand slowed her down.

The water! The salt of the earth is in the water! I'll be safe if I can make it to the water!

But they wanted her before she reached the shoreline. They wriggled beneath her bare feet, growing, larger now, following like sandworms in a movie commercial she'd once seen, ready to lunge up from beneath and take her down.

She tried to move faster but tripped over a man on his blanket and fell, sprawling, into a gathering of little girls making sand cakes. The girls screamed out in fury.

Then they recognized her.

"Mother Claire!"

Leave me alone! Let me get to the water!

Claire pushed herself to her knees.

"Look," cried the man she'd tripped over, "it's Mother Claire! Dear God, she is here!"

Several women rushed over. "Mother Claire, bless us!"

Claire tried to get to her feet but they were around her now, eyes full of wonder and awe and expectation.

"Mother Claire, touch me, please! I've got arthritis in my shoulder!"

"Mother Claire, bless me! Please touch me! My daughter is living in sin and won't come home to us! Please make this better!"

Claire tried again to stand but couldn't. They were around her like hyenas around a zebra. Pressing in. Demanding.

"Mother Claire, my son is atheist! Doesn't that mean he'll go to Hell?"

"Mother Claire, I've got bad eyes, heal me!"

"Mother Claire, my marriage is failing..."

"Mother Claire, my brother is dying..."

Go away! There are devils after me! Can't you see them? Can't you hear them? They want to swallow me! I must get to the sea!

"Mother Claire!"

Claire spit sand and raised her hand to push the people away. But they took it as a sign, cried out in joy, and pressed in even more closely.

"Mother Claire, bless us!"

Beneath her and all around her, shadows cast by her body and those of the crowd were birthing more demons than she'd ever seen before. Snarling faces in the darkness, glinting teeth, strumming claws. The people leaned over her, folded into her to embrace her, and the monsters came, too. They began to rake her skin and slash at her face, snarling, "Tooooooo goooood! Your light was tooooooooo bright and you were blinded!" They punctured her ears and sliced the flesh of her tongue.

And in the moment before they popped her eyes, she saw something in the shadows. She saw a truth she'd never imagined. She saw the hot, devilish core that been born because of her work and her failure to look deeper, to pay attention.

She saw the fraternal order of police in Detroit, who had been in the news as staging parties for homeless children, herding the children off, with the secret approval of the city government, into dark alleys and shooting them quietly, discreetly. The city boasted record child placement and was awarded a "Best City in Which To Live" status.

She saw crack-addicted mothers, paraded in the media as going to newly-established treatment centers which were, in truth, military experimental centers that left some mutilated and most dead.

She saw transient poor, begging dollars at subway entrances, led away by benevolent priests who paused to smile for the paparazzi, kissing the ragged men, and thanking Mother Claire for her inspiration. Then, once the impression was made and the photos were taken, the poor were crammed into tractor trailers and driven under cloak of night to the interior of the Mexican desert and left to their own devices without food or water.

No one would miss any of them. Everyone wanted to think their country had gone Christ-like, and love was worn like a badge for the rest of the world to see.

It's my fault! A small rush of salt water, first of the high tide, flooded beneath her on the sand. Cool. Wet.

God forgive me!

And then she turned her blinded, bloody face away from the crowd atop her, baring her neck for them or for the shadows or for whatever would take her life away.

So the healing could begin.

The Well

Dear Grandmother,

Rick and I drove out to your farmhouse last evening. I didn't really want to go. I hate the place. It scared me as a kid. You scared me as a kid. Even as an adult, I never liked your farmhouse. And I never liked you. The house was creepy. And you were so mean.

We came out to look at your furniture. We had to decide what we would sell at auction. Now that you are in the nursing home, it's time to get rid of it all.

Rick and I parked in the side yard. It's so overgrown. Briars everywhere. Thistles. Weeds. And that piece warped plywood lying over the old well.

I know you were furious that we moved you to the nursing home last week. You were born in the house. You grew up in the house. You were married and had your thirteen children in the house. You never left that property in 94 years. Yes, we tricked you. We told you we were only going to drive you to the edge of the land to see if the river was flooding. We didn't go to the river, of course. Once we got out on the road you stared at us with those ice-cold eyes and said nothing. Later, Rick laughed that it was a good thing you are so small and frail.

We aren't laughing now.

We drove here this evening, parked the truck, and walked through the weeds to the house. The front porch steps creaked. The door squealed. We went into the front hall and tried the light switch. No lights came on.

"Maybe she didn't pay her last bill?" said Rick.

"No," I said. "The place is paid up."

Something skittered on the dark floor beside me. I gasped. "What was that?"

"A mouse?" Rick guessed.

"Do we have a flashlight?" I asked.

There was one in the truck. It was a big one that should have been bright but the battery was old. The light it shined was a sickly yellow.

We went down the hallway to the parlor, where you used to sit in your rocking chair and stare. You do have great antiques, Grandmother. That rocking chair. That old writing desk. That hand-carved table. That chest. That sofa. They were all filthy because you stopped cleaning years ago.

Something rustled near the ceiling. Rick nearly dropped the flashlight. "What was that?"

"Birds?" I guessed.

We looked at the rocking chair. It was worn but otherwise in good shape. We put a green sticker on it, meaning it would go to auction. We looked at the other furniture in the room. Most got green stickers except for two picture frames and a lamp that was falling apart.

Then we checked the desk. It was locked but we found a key taped underneath. Rick pulled the drawer open and something small ran up his arm. He shouted and shook it off.

"What was that?" he cried.

"A spider?" I guessed.

"I hate this place," he said.

"Welcome to the club," I answered.

In the desk was a note, brittle with age. You know it was there, Grandmother. You put it there. You wrote it.

I read it out loud: "To whoever finds this note. You would only be opening my desk if I've been moved out of my house. And so it's time to tell you. I have hid my most precious treasure in the well. Please don't leave it for a stranger to find. It is for family."

"You are the only family member she has left," said Rick.

"She wants me to have her treasure?" I said. "Maybe I misjudged her."

"Maybe," said Rick.

"But it's down in that well," I said. "Eww."

"I wonder what kind of treasure it is?" said Rick. "Money? Jewelry?"

I grinned. "Wouldn't that be great? We should go out and look in the well. It scared me as a kid, but I think I can handle it now."

I looked at the note again, Grandmother. I remembered how much you spooked me with your snarls, your stares. If there was anything I deserved, it was your hidden treasure.

The sky was charcoal gray. The yard was cast in the blue of moonlight. Rick found a crowbar in the back of the truck. We knelt in the weeds beside the old well. As he began to pry up the crusty plywood, something slithered out and into the grass.

"What was that?" shouted Rick.

"I think a snake," I said.

Rick tugged, grunted, and huffed. And then with a crack, the wood flipped over into the briars.

The smell that rose from the well was dreadful. The cold air that drifted upward made me shiver. I leaned over slowly. I shined the flashlight down into the black maw. My hand was shaking. I could see the slime-covered stone walls for several feet and the rest was swallowed in blackness.

"What do you see?" asked Rick.

I saw nothing. There was no rope hanging down that might have a treasure tied to the end. Was something hidden in the stone wall? Or far, far down in the bottom of the well?

The night clouds covered the moon. It was even darker now.

"Well?" asked Rick, leaning over beside me.

I heard a soft clicking sound down in the well.

"What was that?" asked Rick.

"I don't know."

There was another clicking sound. This time it was a little louder.

"Maybe we should wait until morning," Rick said. "I can't see anything."

And then it rushed up and out of the well, its red eyes wide and dreadful. Its mouth wide and wailing, its sharp claws slashing. It caught Rick in the face and took him down. I screamed and grabbed Rick's arm. We scrambled up and raced for the farmhouse. The hideous creature was right behind us, its fiery breath on our necks. Taking two steps at a time we flew up to the porch and through the front door. We slammed it behind us just in time to hear the creature smash into it on the other side.

"What was that?" I cried in the dark hallway. "What was it?"

Rick didn't answer. He slid to the floor, bleeding, panting.

I ran from room to room, locking the windows and then the rear door in the kitchen. My heart pounded. Then I helped Rick into the parlor, where he now lies on your antique sofa.

I am writing this letter by candlelight. I found one in your desk, Grandmother. I want to tell you we found your treasure. It tried to kill us. I can hear it outside the house. It is pacing on the porch, snarling. It's digging at the door and the windows. It is trying to get in.

I knew you never wanted to leave your house. I know now that you were ready in case I did anything against your wishes.

I have a feeling I'll be doing what you had wanted to do. I have a feeling I will never leave this place.

I just heard wood crack. I think it is the front door.

No, we aren't laughing anymore.

Landfill

Marlin County was the western most county in all of Virginia. It covered a steep chunk of the Allegheny Mountains and bordered with Kentucky to the north and Tennessee to the west. There were three towns in Marlin County – Marionville (population 746), Ritter (population 1,092), and the county seat of Darling (population 2,396). Nobody ever moved to Marlin County, few left, most just lived his or her life there then died. Marlin did have its share of spook stories, ancient tales of the ghost of a hunter who wreaked havoc on man and beast alike, and paranormal investigators occasionally came to Marlin in search of something to put on television or in a book. They always left sorely disappointed, however, finding nothing whatsoever except a few abandoned cabins, a couple disintegrating barns, and a single limestone cavern that had caved in long ago. And so with the lack of city comforts and lack of ghosts, tourism was not a big moneymaker in Marlin County.

The Marlin County landfill consisted of fifty-seven acres on Barren Ridge Road. The landfill handled waste from the county residents, accepting bagged and un-bagged trash, recyclable materials and liquids, appliances, bulky waste (also called furniture), cardboard, construction materials, tires, yard waste, and dead animals (which could only be dropped off between noon and 3 p.m., and had to be driven out to the farthest reach of the fill where they were bulldozed as quickly as the dozer guy could get to them.) The landfill took in about 300 tons of waste each day, and it employed nine full time workers.

Kyle Jones had been on the landfill payroll since it opened eight years earlier. And he detested the newest employee, Jack, who had been there a month.

Kyle's job was managing the large "Household Waste" station of the landfill, where county folks hauled their truckloads of bagged and un-bagged trash to toss into the dumpsters. Kyle strode back and forth among the parked vehicles, making sure people were following the rules (no toxic materials, vegetation, or liquids, thank you), helping the elderly fling bags when needed, and rescuing items that residents threw away but which looked to have some value. Kyle scavenged these items – a shovel, a picture frame, a toy that wasn't too molded, dented pots and pans, and the like – and put them into the shed that served as his office. Such was the sole perk of working in a landfill. He made extra money by cleaning up and selling the items at the local flea market. Kyle didn't mind his boss, Jorge Ramirez, and the co-workers stayed out of his way. Things were tolerable at the ole landfill.

Then Jack came along in early June.

Looking at Jack, the last thing you would think was landfill employee. He was all of sixteen, skinny as a stick with a decided limp and one eye bigger than the other. But he'd been hired to help keep the place clean. He hurried around the landfill, from station to station with his push broom and wheeled barrel, smiling an insipid, split-faced smile, chatting up the customers and sweeping up all the loose trash that blew here and there.

After the first week, Kyle asked Jack if he was related to one of the landfill's higher-ups, and Jack had just grinned, shrugged, and said, "Nope. I'm just a good cleaner-upper!"

It wasn't so much the good cleaner-upper aspect of Jack that drove Kyle nuts, (and the lots and decks of the landfill had never looked so tidy, that was true) or even Jack's overly cheerful demeanor (though that could set Kyle's teeth on edge), but the fact that there was now competition for stuff. Not only did Jack sweep, he often found things before Kyle did, stuff Kyle would have loved to sell, and spirited them away to his old Dodge pickup. Jack could swipe a nice-looking bicycle wheel, length of rope, or a perfectly good flowerpot out of a dumpster before Kyle could even get his larger body across the lot to have a look.

Then Jack would trot-limp past Kyle with the goodies under his arm and add it to the stash in his truck bed.

One afternoon, as Jack was pushing his broom across the Household Waste parking lot, whistling some moronic tune, the bulge of something he'd rescued from a dumpster stuffed down the front of his t-shirt. Kyle walked over and grabbed the broom out of Jack's hands.

"What's in your shirt, kid?"

Jack's brows went up. "A beach towel I found."

"Beach towel? We're a million miles from the beach."

"More like five hundred miles," said Jack happily.

Kyle grunted. "A million. Five hundred. Same thing. Point is, why do you need a beach towel?"

"It's nice. It's got a picture of seagulls on it."

Damn it! I want a beach towel with seagulls on it!

Jack reached out. "Can I have my broom back?"

"Just hold on."

Jack folded his arms but kept on smiling.

"Here's the thing," said Kyle, not sure what he was going to say until the words tumbled out of his mouth. "I had a talk with the boss. With Mr. Ramirez. You know Mr. Ramirez?"

"He hired me."

"Well, he said you can't be taking stuff out of the dumpsters anymore."

"Really? He never said that to me."

"He asked me to tell you."

"But you got a few things just this morning, I saw –"

"What you saw was that Mr. Ramirez gave *me* the right to go in the dumpsters since I've been working here a long time. But not you." (Of course, this was not true; Ramirez didn't give two shits as to who might be dumpster diving.)

Jack shrugged and said, "I'll double check with Mr. Ramirez on that. I remember him telling me when he hired me that what people threw away was up for grabs as long as it didn't cause any mess."

Damn it, thought Kyle. *He best not check with Ramirez and have me seen as a liar.* And so he said, "Well, no, never mind. No need to do that. I'll speak with him and make sure it's okay for you to pick up stuff to keep."

Jack nodded cheerfully. "Sure, thanks!"

Crap! thought Kyle. *Backed myself in a corner here.* And so he had to come up with another plan.

Several days passed. Kyle watched with envy as the hobbling yet swift-moving Jack scarfed up a fairly new pair of sneakers, the grate to a barbecue grill, and a tarnished but unbroken brass candlestick, and put them in his truck. All things Kyle could have sold.

I've never seen Jack at the flea market, Kyle thought as he helped a goat farmer hoist broken vinyl siding into a dumpster. *I bet that little weasel just hoards the stuff. What a waste! If I could get my hands on some of what he took, he wouldn't even notice, I betcha!*

But how to get his hands on the stuff the weasel took was the challenge. Jack was too happy and clueless to succumb to threats.

Kyle's grandma used to say, "You catch more flies with honey than with vinegar." And his grandma, a moonshiner who could charm the hell out of, and the pants off of, revenuers, had been one smart cookie.

And so Kyle decided to become Jack's best buddy, as much as that would make his stomach turn. He started chatting Jack up when there was a spare moment.

"Hey there, Jack," Kyle said when Jack passed by his shed, pushing his broom, "where you live, anyway?"

Jack blinked and looked up. "Off Possum Creek Road on Peekers Ridge. Near the old cave."

"That caved-in cave?"

"Yep."

"Black Stone Cave, where people used to say the scary ghost of a dead hunter lived?"

Jack giggled. "Silly people believing in scary ghosts!"

"How long you live up there?"

"Born there. Always lived there."

"Yeah?"

"Yeah."

"What your last name, anyway?"

"Frye."

"Who you live with up there?"

"Don't live with nobody, not since my daddy died last month."

"Your daddy dead?"

"That's what died means."

Kyle bit the inside of his cheek. *What a stupid question.* He said, "I know that. I was kiddin' with you. What was your daddy's first name? Maybe I knew him."

"Johnny-Ray Frye.

"Oh, right," said Kyle. "I do remember Johnny-Ray Frye."

"You knew him?"

"I knew who he was."

"Okay," said Jack with a grin, and he went on with his broom.

I remember old Johnny-Ray, thought Kyle. *Crazy, that one. He was a hoarder, too. Collected things off the side of the road. Rumors say he took all that shit home for some reason. Guess his son takes after him.*

Maybe I can find out where his house is. Get some of the stuff back.

A couple days later, as Kyle stood beside a station wagon where a woman and her children were scooping out big bags of garbage and making a game of tossing them into the dumpsters, he spied Jack passing by with his broom. He lifted his hand and waved.

"Hey, Jack."

Jack stopped and looked over. He waved back.

Kyle left the mom and kids and ambled over to Jack. "Listen carefully. I saw a guy tossing containers of rat poison in a couple of the dumpsters this morning. I tried to stop him but there they went. Don't go picking in the dumpsters 'til I can get them hosed out."

"I don't think so," said Jack.

"Don't think so what?"

"I was sweeping here all morning. I saw everything that got thrown away. I watched carefully like I always do. I saw some jugs of cat litter and plant food that kinda looked like rat poison containers. But no rat poison."

"You just missed it is, all."

"No," said Jack. His grin pissed Kyle off more than ever. "You just made a mistake."

"You sure?" Kyle hated the way that question sounded, like he was giving in to the little weasel, like he was admitting the little weasel was right.

Damn!

"I'm sure," said Jack. And off he went with his broom, limping, whistling and sweeping up the wads of wet newspaper and aluminum cans scattered about the lot.

How Kyle hated the little weasel.

How he hated living in piss-poor Marlin County and having to fight over the scraps in dumpsters.

And how he hated his job and wished he could do something, anything, else.

It was the following Tuesday, when Jack climbed into a dumpster and claimed a great looking area rug damaged only by a mid-sized pee stain, that was the final straw. Kyle wasn't going to let the little weasel get away with taking all the goodies. He thought about taking a sick day when he was sure Jack was working, driving up Possum Creek Road to find the Frye house, breaking in (wearing gloves, of course, to leave no prints, he'd watched plenty of cop shows), and taking back all the goodies he could cram in his Ford.

But as smart as Kyle considered himself, and as un-superstitious as he was, he didn't like the idea of being near Black Stone Cave all by himself. Of *course* there was no such thing as ghosts. Of *course* the cave wasn't haunted. Even those people from the TV networks who'd come with their official night vision goggles, their vibration detectors, and their EMF meters had not found anything, so of course there was nothing to worry about.

But still, the idea gave him the creeps. And so he devised a Plan B.

"Hey there, Jack Frye," said Kyle the next afternoon as Jack loaded up his pickup truck with a broken pitch fork, a cardboard box of books, a stool with two legs, and several decent lengths of pipe.

"Hey," said Jack, smiling.

"You got a lot of stuff today."

"Yep."

"How 'bout I follow you up to your place and help you unload it. I mean, let's be honest, you aren't that big and I can carry heavy stuff easy."

"I do okay," said Jack. "I don't have any trouble carrying stuff."

"Seriously, you're bound to rupture something."

"No, thank you."

Damn you, weasel!

Kyle manufactured a quick Plan C.

"Listen," he said, "I was thinking about your dad the other day. I thought I hadn't met him but then I remembered, yeah, I met him in Darling one morning."

"I don't think my daddy ever went into Darling."

"Oh, maybe it was Marionville."

"Don't think he ever went into Marionville, either."

"Hold on, it was Ritter. That's right, we met in Ritter a couple years ago. Your daddy did go into Ritter sometimes, didn't he?"

"Well, he got us groceries in Ritter, sometimes."

"That's right! Groceries. We met at the grocery store. He told me he liked to collect things from the road. I told him I worked at the landfill. He said he had a nice son."

"My daddy was a mute," said Jack.

Fuck!

"What I mean is he kinda signed that to me, about you being a nice son. I'm smart, I can pick up on things like that. Signs and all."

"Really?"

Fuck fuck fuck!

"Anyway, I'd like to pay my respects."

"What do you mean?" asked Jack.

"Come up to your place, bring a wreath for his grave. You buried him at home, didn't you?" *Please say you buried him at home.*

"We don't belong to the Baptist or Methodist Church," said Jack. "So yeah, I buried him at home."

"Well, that's just fine. Could I follow you home this afternoon? Bring a wreath?"

"I suppose that would be all right. You got good tires?"

"The best," said Kyle.

"You got a wreath?"

"I'll have one by quitting time."

Nobody threw away a decent artificial wreath that afternoon, so Kyle took his twenty-minute break to leave the landfill, drive like crazy to the Baptist Church, grab a wreath off a grave, then drive like crazy back to the landfill.

The landfill closed at 4:30 p.m., after which the employees made their final investigations, ran the compactors one last time and buried the last of the bury-ables. Then everyone went home at 6:00. Jack climbed into his Dodge (with his excellent goodies), Kyle into his Ford (with a few mediocre goodies), and they left the grounds for Barren Ridge Road.

Jack was a very slow driver, as if he had nothing else to do in his life but go back and forth from the landfill. Which was probably the case. Kyle tried not to tailgate but it was all he could do to keep back a bit.

Stupid weasel! Hurry up! It's getting dark!

But if all went as planned, Kyle would not only be able to retrieve some of the best goodies that should have been his, Jack would no longer be any competition. Not that Kyle was planning on killing Jack; Kyle wasn't quite ready to do something like that. But Kyle was going to tell Jack some things in confidence that would make the weasel reconsider his place of employment. Tell Jack how the some of the other employees hated him and were planning on staging an accident that would mess him up in ways he couldn't imagine. Tell him that Kyle had tried to talk the employees out of it, but they didn't like Jack's mannerisms, his constant grins, and the fact that he was making as much as they were for doing nothing more than pushing a broom. Kyle would, as a friend, tell Jack it would be best he never return. He'd also tell Jack that if he wanted the other employees to leave him alone completely, to never come up to his house to teach him a lesson, Jack best return most of the items he'd taken from the dumpsters. Kyle would distribute the goodies to the others as a peace offering.

Up the winding Barren Ridge Road through the dense forest of the mountainside, passing the occasional small farm, weedy field, sagging barn and house. Night was beginning to settle on the mountain.

Hurry up, weasel!

Then Jack took a left onto the pot-holed Possum Creek Road and continued on another mile. Possum Creek Road had once been a Native American hunting trail and it was little more than that, still. Mostly mud, patches of gravel, bedrock. Kyle kept up, telling himself all this would be worth it.

The trees were even thicker now, and the shadows darker. Branches bent over the road, locking with each other, creating the sense of being in a tunnel. Or a cave. The road became more ragged now, with trenches and angles and stumps protruding. The climb was even steeper.

At last a small, tar-brick house appeared in a clearing to the right. Jack steered into the yard. Kyle parked behind him. He got out, dragging the wreath with him, and made a quick study of the place. Visible behind the house was more mountain, continuing on up and up. The front yard was filled with thistle. The windows of the house were cracked and the front porch sagging. And yet, in spite of what Kyle had expected, there was not a single piece of junk on the porch or in the yard, only an empty wheeled cart and a birdbath standing at a tilt.

Stuff must be crammed inside the house along with the crap Johnny-Ray collected.

Jack hopped from his Dodge and headed for the wheeled cart. Kyle held up his hand.

"First," he said, "let me pay my respects to your daddy."

Jack's eyes opened wide and he smiled. "Oh, yes, of course. Sorry!"

Jack led Kyle around the house to the backyard – a lumpy, weedy pasture on the far side of which was the steep mountain rise. A dark dot punctuated the base of that rise. It was a cave. Black Stone Cave.

Damn!

Twilight had settled hard, and Kyle nearly tripped over the plain stone marker that indicated the grave.

"That's where I buried my daddy," said Jack. "Put your wreath down and I can get back to my duty."

Kyle tried to look solemn, bowed his head for a second then dropped the wreath over the stone marker. He turned to Jack and said, "I got to talk to you about the other employees at the landfill. What they said about –"

But Jack didn't hear him. He was already limping quickly back around the house. Kyle followed to find Jack taking the broken stool out of the back of the truck and placing it in the wheeled cart.

"Jack, hold on and listen to me," Kyle said, but Jack reached in for the broken pitchfork, and added it to the cart.

"Jack, seriously, listen to me. This is important."

Jack pulled the cardboard box of books from the back of the truck.

Kyle grabbed Jack by the arm and shook him. Two of the books popped up and out of the box. Jack gasped.

"Would you listen to me?" said Kyle. "You have to return all the stuff you've taken. The other guys, well, you haven't heard them talking like I have. And it ain't good."

Jack giggled. "Silly! I can't take anything back."

"Yes, you can. You're...you're in danger. We need to go into your house and get everything and take it all back.

We can take several trips if need be. The guys at the landfill are really mad at you, and –"

"I can't take anything back," said Jack. He scooped up the books from the grass, put them back in the box, and put the box in the wagon. "I don't have the stuff anymore."

"Of course you do. You've taken lots of stuff. Don't lie to me. It's in your house, isn't it?"

"No."

"Then where is it?"

"I said I don't have it anymore."

Kyle stormed over to the porch, up to one of the front window, and peered inside. All he could see was a single rocking chair, a bed, and a table. He went to the other window, and inside saw only a woodstove, some shelves stocked with a few canned foods, and a straight-back chair.

"How many rooms you got in this house?" he demanded.

"Two," said Jack.

"Where's the stuff? Seriously, Jack, I don't have time for your shit! I mean you don't have time to ignore my warning!"

"Oh, go on home, Kyle," said Jack, smiling. "You paid your respects."

"Hold on. Wait. At least give me back the stuff you got today. Can you at least do that?"

"I need it."

"You don't need it, you just want it!"

Jack's persistent smile suddenly vanished. But instead of looking angry, he seemed sad. "Go home, Kyle."

Kyle grabbed for the wagon. With surprising strength, Jack pushed him back. Kyle grabbed again; again, Jack pushed him back.

"Go home," said Jack.

Kyle clenched his teeth. He didn't want to fight the weasel. But he didn't come all the way up here, banging up his shocks, wasting his time, for no good reason. Where was the damn stuff?

Kyle got into his Ford and slammed the door shut. He spun the vehicle around, drove off the yard, and down Possum Creek Road a short distance. Then he stopped. Got out. Marched back to Jack's house and hid behind a sycamore, where, with the help of the glow of a half-moon, he could watch what was going on. There was no shed or barn in which Jack put the stuff, but clearly the stuff was going somewhere. Things didn't just vanish into thin air. If Kyle could see where it went, then he could wait and get it after Jack went to bed. It was now as much about the goodies as it was about winning.

Even though it's nighttime now.

I hate the dark.

I hate the dark up here near that damned cave!

I hate the weasel!

Kyle watched as Jack adjusted the goodies in the wheeled cart then pulled it back behind the house. Kyle sprinted across the front yard, around the side of the house, and peered out to see Jack crossing the weedy field with the wagon bouncing behind him. Moving toward the mountain wall.

Toward the cave.

Kyle's heart picked up a faster rhythm.

It's not haunted, don't be stupid, Kyle. You're a grown man, so just cut it out.

There was a small cedar in the center of the field; Kyle scooted across to hide behind it. Closer now. Kyle squinted through the darkness. He saw Jack stop at the mouth of the cave and begin to take the goodies out and place them on the ground.

What the hell is the weasel doing? Does he hide stuff inside the fucking cave? And I thought his daddy was weird!

Kyle swallowed hard. He licked his dried lips.

No way am I going to try to get the stuff out of there. Tomorrow, when the weasel comes in to work, I'll use Plan D. Convince Ramirez to fire him. I can do that! I might not get my stuff back, but there'll be no more weasel taking what should be mine!

Kyle hunched over and turned to leave.

Jack called, "I know you're back there. C'mon then, might as well have a look."

Kyle stopped, caught his breath. "This isn't me. I'm not here." *Damn, what's wrong with me?*

Jack laughed.

"I'm just kidding."

"Sure. Come on over here."

I can't let him know I'm afraid. Hell, I'm not afraid. I don't believe any of those stupid stories about a ghost in the cave. That's nonsense.

Kyle held his head high (*I'm not afraid I'm not afraid!*) and walked over the field to the cave. He stopped beside Jack and crossed his arms. Though it was quite dark, he could see inside the maw, see that the cave was empty with just a wall of crumbled stone fifteen or so yards inside.

"My daddy gathered things off the side of the road," said Jack. "So did my granddaddy. My great-granddaddy went to houses at night and took things from their trash. Luckily nobody ever heard him and shot him! Ha! I'm not sure what my great-great granddaddy did but he collected things, too. Getting a job at the landfill made it a lot easier for me, that's for sure." Jack ginned, giggled.

It's too dark out here! Kyle fumbled in his pocket; he almost always carried a penlight with him. But his pocket was empty. He'd left the light in his Ford.

Jack said, "Okay, now, don't move, Kyle."

There was a soft rustling from inside the cave. At first it sounded like bats, but no, the rustling was too much, too intense. The rustling was followed by a low moan.

Oh no no, I didn't hear that!

Kyle didn't want to look but he couldn't help himself. A pale light flickered in the cave, back at the crumbled stone wall. The moaning grew louder, rising in pitch, becoming a wail.

Kyle clenched his fists. His breathing picked up. He stepped back. *What the hell is this?*

The pale light grew brighter. It floated toward the mouth of the cave, taking shape, developing a hideous face with eyes that burned scarlet and arms that swirled and flapped.

Oh shit shit shit! Kyle stumbled back another step, tripped on his feet, and dropped on his ass.

The brightly-glowing ghost reached the front of the cave. It opened its mouth wide, emitting a horrific, deafening shriek. Its arms flailed about in the air as if ready to strike.

Jack laughed and said, "Here you go! Here are your treasures!" He pointed at the goodies on the ground. The ghost's dreadful head tipped back and forth as if considering each one. Then it reached out with its arms, lifted the whole pile, raised them to its mouth, opened wide, and swallowed them whole. And they were gone, as if they'd never existed.

The ghost burped. It smiled a ghastly, ghostly smile.

Jack laughed and reached out as if to pet it.

What the hell? thought Kyle.

Then the ghost spun around several times, screaming in what seemed like delight, and then withdrew into the cave. The screams became moans then went silent. The bright light became pale then winked out.

Kyle, on his ass, just stared.

Jack giggled.

"What was that? What happened?" asked Kyle, his voice stripped down into a whisper.

"He's my pet."

"What?"

"It's the hunter. Was the hunter, I mean." Jack grinned. "He's been in there since the cave-in a couple hundred years ago. He was hunting treasure and ended up suffocating, I think it was, or crushed. Either way, he died. As in dead, you know."

"Yeah, I know." *Weasel!*

"For a while, long ago, he got out and haunted people. Didn't mean to scare them but I'm sure you know that most people don't like ghosts. These people tried to catch him, to hurt him, to be rid of him once and for all. Isn't that sad? But when my family moved here, we started bringing him treats – treasures. He's not picky about what I bring him. He thinks it's all treasure. He likes it all. So while the stories of a ghost are true, they're really old stories. The ghost hasn't haunted folks since my family decided to help him."

Kyle stood slowly, frowning, staring between the weasel and the now-empty cave.

"Even those ghost hunters can't detect him," said Jack. "He stays far enough back so they can't record anything."

Kyle rubbed his chin. "So, you're saying the ghost is happy, just taking – eating – things you scavenge for him?"

"Yeah!"

"What if you stopped bringing him goodies?"

Jack giggled. "I can't think about that, for how sad would that be? But don't be silly. I'll do my duty and keep him happy. I'll always bring him treasures, that's for sure."

Kyle nodded.

He and Jack went back across the field without another word. Jack went into his house. Kyle walked down to his Ford, climbed in, and began the bumpy, uncomfortable drive back down the mountain.

The weasel might not want to think about what might happen if he no longer cared for the ghost. But Kyle didn't mind. What if Jack actually did have a major accident at work? Someone else would have to take over and bring treasures to the ghost up in Black Stone Cave. And then, that someone would spread the word that the ghost was back on the scene. This would encourage ghost hunters to return and excitement and tourism would pick up. That someone could move into the abandoned house on Possum Creek Road and offer "watch the ghost eat junk" tours for a nice fee, get on TV, maybe even write a book. That someone would become the Marlin County man of the hour. That someone could quit the landfill and stop with the damned dumpster diving.

So much to consider.

Time for Plan E.

The Replacement

Two things were on her mind. The plaque on the floor at the back of the closet that read, "Daughters are Forever" and the fact that she'd noticed that her fingernails grew much too quickly. Yes, of course, there were more things to think about, to commit to memory and to behavior, but as Tracey stepped into the bathroom to brush her teeth on her first morning as the McCauleys' replacement, those were the things that stuck in her head.

Daughters are forever. What an unfortunate plaque, and for them to have kept it.

The girl who used to own these hands must have had to trim the nails every few days.

Tracey ran the water, put paste on the toothbrush. Brushed carefully. She'd been told her teeth might come loose if she wasn't careful.

"Tracey?"

It was Mrs. McCauley – Mom – out in the bedroom.

"Yes?"

"Come out here, please. Tracey."

Tracey put the toothbrush down and checked to make sure no teeth had dropped into the sink. She almost forgot to put her robe on before leaving the bathroom, which would have been a mistake. Parents don't want to see their fourteen-year-old replacement naked. The long, savage scars would have been more shocking than breasts or pubic hair.

Mr. and Mrs. McCauley – Dad and Mom – were waiting there, by her bed with its pink and white spread and lacy pillow shams, watching her with a mixture of awe, anger, hope, and sadness.

Tracey tied her robe and smiled her best smile. "Yes?"

"We just wanted to see you," said Mom. "To make sure this was real."

Dad frowned at his wife; embarrassed, maybe? "No, that's not it. Of course this is real. We just wanted to see you in the daylight is all. Stand by the window. Open the curtains. Let's have a look."

Tracey did as she was asked, saying nothing, letting her new parents have a look. Dad sniffed, crossed his arms, and nodded. *He wants to like me,* Tracey thought. Mom cried a little then wiped her nose and said, "It's time for breakfast. Get dressed and we'll see you downstairs."

"All right. Thank you," said Tracey.

Mom and Dad nodded, left the room. Tracey looked in the dresser, finding jeans and baggy t-shirt. She slipped them on along with a thick pair of socks, and went downstairs down to the kitchen.

"Hugs. Though you will feel no affection for them, you must offer them hugs," Dr. Chatham at the Replacement Shop had told Tracey before the McCauleys came to pick her up. Marla, the McCauley's real daughter, had been a real hug bug. A hug bug who loved French toast, all shades of pink, Siamese kittens, a boy at school named Fredrick, and her parents.

Daughters are Forever.

Until they aren't.

Until they overdose on some vicious recreational drug cocktail at an unsupervised birthday party, collapse, and die behind the sofa. Found the next morning when the mother of the birthday girl starts vacuuming.

The Replacement Shop's motto was simple: "We can help your transition." They had a colorful brochure: "The Stages of Grief and How the Replacement Shop Can Help," complete with representative photos showing parents in shock and denial, pain, anger, bargaining, depression, reconstruction/replacement, initial recovery, and then, finally, acceptance. On the back were the prices. Tracey was a mid-list replacement, guaranteed to last six months. This was to be enough of a cushion for the McCauleys to move into the stage of acceptance or at least initial recovery.

Down in the kitchen, Dad was opening a food pouch and dumping out several waffles onto a plate. Mom was sitting at the table, folding and refolding a napkin. Tracey gave Dad a hug around his waist. He tensed but then hugged her back. Then Tracey went to Mom with a hug around the neck. Mom did not hug her back.

That was certainly to be expected. It was only the first full day. There was time.

Breakfast was a bowl of rice cereal and orange cut into little slices. It was tasteless, just as the technicians at the Shop had told her it would be. It didn't matter. Her function wasn't to enjoy food. *Just be careful with the teeth*, she thought. *Don't bite anything too hard with the incisors.*

The molars are probably okay but don't chance it.

#

When breakfast was done, Mom took Tracey shopping.

"Normally," Mrs. McCauley said as they climbed onto the airtram at the corner of Freeman and Cole, "I would do my shopping from home. Most everybody does, of course. Why go out when you can stay in? But I can't select my new hair without trying it out first, so I prefer to go to the salon."

Tracey nodded. She sat beside Mom with her hands in her lap. "Talk to them," Dr. Chatham at the Replacement Shop had instructed Tracey. "Not much, but don't sit around like a simple-minded idiot. Yet don't overdo it, either. Your job is to help them get through their loss. Just do as we instructed you to do. Do you understand?"

Tracey had understood. *Talk. Don't sit around like a simple-minded idiot. Don't overdo it.*

"That's a pretty dog," Tracey said, pointing to a small poodle in the lap of a woman in a seat nearby.

Mom stiffened in the seat beside her. "Marla hated dogs."

"I didn't know that. No one told me. I'm sorry."

"Don't mention dogs to me again, or to Mr....to Dad."

"I won't."

"Marla liked cats."

"Okay. I'm sorry."

Mom stared at Tracey, her eyebrows drawing together, then apart, as if wondering if she had done the right thing in buying Tracey.

Don't sit around like a simple-minded idiot. She blurted out, "I love you."

Why did I say that? Tracey blinked, stunned at her words.

Mom's eyes widened and then filled with stunned tears. "You can't. Don't say that!"

"I'm so sorry." Tracey reached out for Mom and touched her shoulder. She wasn't supposed to feel affection for the McCauleys, but for some reason, she had felt something for Mom. "Please forgive me!"

Mom's tears spilled and she wiped them away before anyone else on the metro could see. Then she straightened in her seat and said, "Well, then. Three stops is the salon. We get off there. Tie your shoes, they've come undone."

#

In spite of its bright and appealing brochure, The Replacement Shop wasn't a government-sanctioned enterprise. It wasn't illegal but it wasn't fully approved. The Shop was located in the basement of The Clone Corporation, the "red-headed stepchild" (so nicknamed by Doctor Reginald Chatham, who ran the Shop) to the certified provider upstairs. The Clone Corp. was fine wine, Dr. Chatham laughed, while The Replacement Shop was a glass of decent beer. But for those who wanted what it offered, it was the best and only option. While The Clone Corp. catered to the grieving rich, creating new children from the DNA of those who had died, The Replacement Shop offered temporary replacements, crafted with a good amount of skill, that lasted at the very least six months, some up to a year.

Tracey – a newly created replacement – had stood in her temporary cooling cell on the evening she was to be picked up, watching and listening as Dr. Chatham explained the finer details of replacements to Mrs. and Mr. McCauley. The couple had called on recommendation of their family therapist, and had come in for their replacement just five days after Marla had been cremated and dispersed.

Chatham told the McCauleys, "Children who lose a beloved pet are often given stuffed animals to hold onto, to hug, to hit, to throw, or just cry over, until the children can come to terms with their sadness. Stuffed animals, as we know, aren't the real thing. And they don't last. But they can help immensely. Our company's rationale is the same. We offer a transitional product to help families over the roughest time in their lives. We have many satisfied customers."

Mrs. McCauley, a small woman with thinning black hair, had asked meekly, "How do we....what do we..." Her voice trailed.

Chatham had put a kindly hand on her hand. "Each replacement has been constructed and trained to be a helpmeet and a comfort. You and your husband merely take yours home, give her space, and refer to our users' guide if you have any issues or concerns."

"Joan," said Mr. McCauley, drawing his wife close. "We discussed this. We placed the order. This is a good thing."

Mrs. McCauley nodded vaguely. Chatham took Tracey from her cell and presented her to her new owners. Family, he called them, a word that struck the newly-assembled Tracey as both odd and sad. "Tracey is now part of your transitional family," he had said. "I wish you all the best as you move through this next phase of your lives."

Neither adult looked at Tracey as they led her away, but she'd been told that would be the norm at first.

#

At her therapist's suggestion, Mrs. McCauley – Mom – agreed to teach Tracey how to bake cookies. The goal was to help Mom move from always thinking of the fun she had baking with Marla to reclaiming the joy of baking. Marla had loved cooking, had loved baking, and her specialty was cookies. Mr. McCauley – Dad – had bragged to his co-workers that his daughter would be a famous chef someday, even though, he admitted to Tracey, Marla was really only good with cookies; more often than not her breads fell and her scones burned.

Mom moved about the kitchen as Tracey sat on a tall stool and watched, knowing she should be helping but not knowing what to do. There was some vague memory of cooking, baking, of stirring with a spoon and sliding pans into an oven. Most likely the girls, or one of the girls, whose brains had been surgically connected to make her brain had enjoyed cooking, baking. They made Tracey feel unsteady at times, these random traces of memories that were supposed to have been bleached out at the Shop. Dr. Chatham had told Tracey she might encounter occasional thoughts, but that she was to ignore them. "Let them go," he had said. "They're just residue. Do you job as you were taught."

Mom brought eggs, flour, sugar, and milk to the counter where Tracey sat. Mom opened the egg carton. "Crack three eggs into the bowl. Then beat them with the whisk. It's the old-fashioned way to make cookies. It's how Marla and I always did it."

"All right," said Tracey. She picked up an egg, cracked it against the side of the bowl. Some of the white slid down the outside but the rest went inside. Mom said nothing. Tracey cracked the other two eggs more successfully. She took the whisk and beat the eggs carefully. Mom whirled her hand in the air to indicate she was to whisk much more quickly. Tracey did.

After the flour, sugar, and milk were added, Mom opened a bag of chocolate chips. "Chocolate chip cookies were Marla's favorite," she said to the bag. "She loved the smell and the taste, even the look of them."

"I know she loved them," said Tracey, and Mom slapped her soundly, planting a red mark on Tracey's face.

"How would you know that?" cried Mom. "How would you know what Marla loved? Don't try to please me with lies!"

Tracey didn't know how she knew, but she knew, deep inside. She said, "I'm so sorry, Mom."

Mom threw the bag of chocolate chips across the room. They sprayed up and out of the bag and landed on the floor, in the sink, on the table. "And I hate that you are supposed to call me Mom! Marla called me Mom! She was my daughter, not you!"

"I'm so sorry."

Mom sat in the middle of the floor. She picked a chocolate chip, looked at it, and then threw it down. She seemed to have deflated, like a popped balloon. "I'm hollow," she said at last.

Tracey looked down at Mom.

"There's a hole in me. Right here." Mom pointed to her chest. "Look! Right here. I don't know how to fill that hole. Having you here is a distraction, it's not a solution!"

"I'm so, so sorry."

"How can you be sorry? You're a freak, you're nothing more than a combination of those who were and who aren't anymore! Don't tell me you're sorry!"

Tracey no longer told Mom she was sorry. Even though she was.

#

Days passed. Dad took Tracey to a battleball game at Game Dome. They sat side by side on the bleachers as Dad's favorite team, the Hammerheads, chased their opponents, the Steelmen, down the field, got control of the ball, and subdued the Steelmen with their clubs. It was a strange game; the players seemed more angry than happy to be playing the sport. Tracey had nothing in her brain to make sense of it, and so she sat and watched and clapped and booed when Dad did. She broke off three of her fast-growing fingernails while clapping, broke them off below the quick, and there was a faint sensation but it didn't hurt.

After the game, as they filed out of the Dome, Dad said, "Marla liked to get ice cream."

"Okay, " said Tracey. "That would be nice."

They walked to a gaily-painted stand and Dad got two cones. His was butter pecan. Tracey's was strawberry. As they walked they ate. There was no real flavor to the ice cream but it did feel cold on Tracey's tongue.

Dad took a bite of his cone and said, "I think you're okay, Tracey. I think a replacement is a good idea. I miss Marla more than I could ever imagine, but it's nice to have a young person...I mean a young replacement...to talk to in her place. You'll never be Marla, but I know that and having you to go to the games with and eat ice cream with is all right."

A replacement, not a person. Tracey nodded. Dad was right about that. Tracey was not a person per say, but rather a well-formed unit from the body parts of many recently deceased young people, body parts that had been donated prior to burial or cremation. Hands from one, legs and feet from others, head, brain, internal organs, all harvested and recompiled by well-trained specialists. Tracey knew what she was. She knew her job and how things would end.

When their ice cream was finished, Dad took Tracey back home. Mom was in the living room, curled up on the sofa. She took one look at Tracey, jumped to her feet, and smashed Tracey head with a marble ashtray.

"I hate you, I hate you!" she screamed.

Dad took Tracey up to her room. He was shaking. He told Tracey it was best she go on to bed. He told her Mom was doing what was expected and hoped Tracey wasn't hurt too badly.

"I didn't really feel it," said Tracey.

"Good night, Tracey."

"Good night, Dad."

A flush filled Tracey's chest.

I love you.

#

The days became a week, became a month. Dad took Tracey to games at the Dome and she clapped and cheered along with him. Fingernails snapped but that didn't matter.

When they ate ice cream, one of Tracey's bicuspids and one of her canines fell out, but she just spit them away and didn't tell Dad. He seemed content to have Tracey along, perhaps he was already healing or maybe in a dream state and she didn't want to chance upsetting him. She gave him hugs when it seemed he was receptive and she learned enough about battleball to hold short conversations about the teams, the plays, the scores.

Mom ignored Tracey most of the time, ordering her to stay up in her bedroom and out from underfoot, but twice a week took her to the yoga studio, where men and women in bright leotards stretched and bent and hummed along to flute music piped in through the walls. Mom told Tracey that Marla had just started learning yoga and it was Tracey's job to try it, too. The first time Tracey put on Marla's bright pink leotard and came out of the dressing room, the women and men saw her scarred body and gasped in revulsion. But then they circled Mom and told her how they hoped the replacement was helping and hadn't Marla been the sweetest daughter ever? Tracey found yoga to be nearly impossible. Her arms and legs did not want to do what the instructor told the class to do, and bending in certain ways made her feel strangely dizzy.

On the airtram on the way to and from the studio, Mom alternated staring at Tracey and staring out the window. Dr. Chatham had said to Tracey, "Everyone's journey through grief is different. Don't take anything personally. Your job is to be whatever the family needs you to be." And so Tracey tried not to worry about Mom. To let her be as she would be.

Though she knew she loved her.

She was not supposed to, and she did not know why she did, but she did.

#

The summer crawled along. One Sunday afternoon, the McCauleys and Tracey traveled by tram out of the city to the Eternal Remembrance Memorial Park and Crematory. Mom and Dad and Tracey walked without speaking through the flowering shrubs and shady trees, past row and rows of gold disks set in the ground until they came to the one on which Marla's name was engraved.

"I brought you a chocolate chip cookie, Honey," said Dad, and he took a cookie from his pocket and placed it on the gold disk. It broke into three pieces when he put it down, and this made Mom cry. Dad took Mom's hand. Then he took Tracey's hand. He squeezed them both gently.

Mom took a pink ribbon from her pocket and put it down beside the cookie. "I saw this at the hair salon and took a bit for you, Sweetie," said Mom. "No replacement will ever take your place. I would kill her in a heartbeat to have you back for just one minute."

Tracey's chest grew tight and she looked away until she could bring herself back around.

Don't take anything personally. Your job is to be whatever the family needs you to be.

#

Four months, and the connection that held Tracey's right arm to her shoulder had begun to loosen and the nerves and muscles were no longer dependable. She did her best to keep Mom and Dad from noticing, though Dad found out quickly when she was no longer able to clap at the games. That was the first and only time Tracey saw Dad break down and cry. He tried to hide it, mopped his face with his bandana as if he were only wiping away sweat, but she could tell by the heaving of his shoulders that he was weeping.

Tracey's heart clenched. She did not want him to hurt, did not want him to suffer. She reached out her left hand and patted his arm. It did not seem to help, for he kept crying, harder now. But she kept patting.

#

Five and a half months into the replacement, Tracey knew it was over. Neither arm worked well, her hearing was fading, and all her teeth were gone. Mom stopped taking Tracey to yoga but had not stopped slapping her when she felt overwhelmed or sending her to her bedroom to have her out of the way. To use Dr. Chatham's lingo, Mom had yet to "turn a corner," but then again, not everyone did or could in six months. Dad, however, was beginning to heal and even smiled genuine smiles now and then.

Tracey had been prepared for it to end, she had been told how easy it would be, but she loved the McCauleys and when she thought about the few weeks that remained she found it almost impossible to bear. Yet she said nothing to Mom and Dad. That was not her job. That would confuse them. That would make things worse.

Lying in bed, staring at the moonlight on the floor, Tracey thought about her impermanence. Every part of her had already served a purpose for another young girl. Every part of her had been recycled and reprogrammed, had been rescued and given a few more months to function. One could not ask for more, but to squeeze a little more from something that had been put to rest.

Brain. Hands. Legs. Feet. Organs. Arms. From grieving parents willing to let the bodies of their children benefit others by donating what had been theirs.

Who had been her beneficiaries for this short experience with the McCauleys? Had any replacement ever wondered? Would it matter to know, before falling into total and permanent disrepair?

Without permission and with the remaining strength in her legs, Tracey left the McCauleys' house after breakfast the following morning while Dad was working in his den and Mom was doing yoga stretches in the living room. With Mom's pass, Tracey climbed aboard the airtram. Passengers gave her wide berth; they knew what she was, what was wrong with her, and the last thing they wanted to be reminded of was dead children.

Tracey rode the tram six stops up to the Replacement Shop. She did not plan to stay there long; she only wanted to ask one question of Dr. Chatham and then she would go home to the McCauleys.

She shuffled around to the back of The Clone Corp., faced the scanner, and identified herself as a replacement belonging to Dr. Chatham in the basement. After a few second, the door opened, allowing her to enter.

She went downstairs.

A couple was in the bright, colorful reception room, sitting in the comfortable chairs, listening to the doctor explain his brochure and give his spiel. Both women turned, stared at Tracey, at the deteriorating body before them, and recoiled both audibly and visibly.

"Is this what we'll get?" asked one.

"Is that how our son will look once we take him home?" asked the other. "Oh, I think not!"

Dr. Chatham was quite displeased; he begged the women to wait and he ushered Tracey into the hall and pushed her against the wall.

"What are you doing here?" he whispered furiously. "Did the McCauleys send you back? Did you run away?"

Tracey leaned against the wall, panting. Her legs shook, preparing to give way.

"Where did I come from?" she managed.

"You know very well that doesn't matter!"

"Did any part of me come from the Eternal Remembrance Memorial Park?"

"Why the hell would you care? You're nothing, you're a stuffed animal, a piece of candy, you are a bit of snow, holding together during the coldest winter then melting when winter is done."

"Tell me.

"No! Now be gone! I've got business!"

"Do you ever take parts that aren't donated?"

"What?"

"Do you ever take parts without permission? Do you ever steal them?"

Dr. Chatham's eyes widened. "Who would think that? Did the McCauleys say that?"

Tracey swallowed hard. "If you do not tell me the truth, I will scream."

Dr. Chatham snarled, stunned by the challenge.

"With every ounce I have left," said Tracey, "I will scream so those women will hear me. I will scream that you steal parts, that you lie and cheat. The women will run from here and word will spread. You will be shut down."

"Bitch!" said Dr. Chatham. "You can do no such thing."

"With every ounce I have left, I will do it." Tracey's hips gave way and she slid to the floor. "I swear."

"Dr. Chatham?" called one of the women. "Are you coming back? Should we leave?"

"I'll be right back!" Dr. Chatham called.

"I'll do it," said Tracey.

"All right," said the doctor, his lip hitching in dismissive disgust. "I will answer you. For what can it matter now as you are coming to pieces? Yes, sometimes we come up short. Sometimes we take what is not donated, because who is to know? What difference can it make? Officials at the Memorial Park help us at times. Rescuing a part here or there before the rest of the child is cremated. What is the problem with that?"

Tracey nodded. She now knew what she had suspected. She licked her lips and her tongue fell away. She tried to stand but could not.

Dr. Chatham pushed the call button on his wrist and a lab assistant came into the hall. "Take her, dispose of her."

"She's still alive, sir."

"To the incinerator, now," said the doctor, and he went into the reception room and slammed the door shut.

Tracey was hoisted over he assistant's shoulder and carried to the far end of the basement where, in a low-ceilinged boiler room, defunct replacements lay in bits and pieces upon a tarp. Tracey was tossed on top of the others.

As she waited her turn in the fire, she felt sad. Sad because Mom and Dad would not know what happened to her. Sad because she loved them and did not want either one to worry.

Sadness.

Love.

Two feelings a replacement was not to experience and yet she did.

It was Marla's heart that had made that happen. Of that, Tracey was certain. Marla's heart, scavenged before cremation and given unknowingly to her temporary stand in. Marla's heart, a heart that had adored her parents more than anything else in her life.

If there was any goodness to this, it was that Mom and Dad had been twice loved, and loved deeply.

Tracey's turn came and she was tossed into the fire. And it did not hurt.

About the Author

Elizabeth Massie is a ninth generation Virginian who lives with her husband, illustrator Cortney Skinner, in the Shenandoah Valley. She writes horror, media tie-ins, historical fiction, poetry, spiritual nonfiction, and educational materials. Her novelette "Stephen," and her novel *Sineater* have won Bram Stoker Awards. Her novelization *The Tudors: Thy Will Be Done* won a Scribe Award. In her spare time she loves exploring, geocaching, knitting, and watching Svengoolie on MeTV. She drinks chai, thinks cheese is beyond nasty, and finds the beach to be the most relaxing place on Earth.

Made in the USA
Las Vegas, NV
23 March 2021

20061757R00125